Other Books in This Series

The Bastard Dragon

Dragon Astray
The Covert Dragons Book 2

By

Viola Grace

Trin has trained to be stealthy, trained to defend herself, but when a bounty on her head threatens the safety of her friends, she has to get out of town.

Visiting a friend and mixing business with her escape, she learns that dragons mixing their bloodlines may be more common than anyone thought.

She spends enough time in Breaker City ordering tea and ceramics to figure out what she wants to do next, and what she wants to do is find out who and where she came from.

Learning the details of her family tree leaves her shaken, but nothing can hold her back when it comes to following her instincts. Not even the very folk she came to meet.

Chapter One

The fist came at her head, and Trin didn't duck. She deflected the attack and struck her opponent with an uppercut that knocked it back.

Rish staggered back and shook her head before flexing her jaw and grinning. "Very good. Let's take a break."

Trin nodded and inclined her head. "Would you like some tea?"

"Water with lemon, please." Rish sighed and headed for the small table and chairs set against one wall of the sub-basement. "You are very fast."

Trin chuckled and poured the water

for her trainer. "I have always been quick. It is a handy skill at an orphanage full of shifters when you are human."

Rish rubbed her jaw. "Well, you are definitely all dragon now. How are you feeling?"

"Good. I love learning things, and these skills are just up my alley." She glanced down at the boiler suit-type clothing that she was wearing. "I also like ditching the skirts now and then."

They sat down and looked around the exercise space that had been created out of a reading room. Training ladies for combat wasn't something that the dragons liked to do. Training an un-mated crystal dragon would have horri-fied most of the population. Lucky for Trin, the hunters and the council head had a plan for her.

She sat back and sipped her water, feeling the slight ache in her hands, back, and feet. In the mornings, she fought Rish; in the afternoons, she got espionage training from Brommin. Today's lesson was going to be memory and assessment. If they had time, there would be some sparring, but her clothing had to be that of a lady. Fighting in a floor-length gown and a corset was not pleasant, but the practice was rather fun, especially when he wrapped his arms around her from behind and his mother had to intervene. He wasn't allowed to fight with her unless Rish was there to hit the brakes.

"So, can I know what you are training me for?" Trin kept asking.

Rish gave her a bland look. "You are being trained for a situation you are uniquely qualified to be in."

"You say that every day."

"And every day for the last three weeks, you have asked me the same question. I am wondering at your ability to learn, Trin."

Trin grinned. "I prefer to think of it as determination and a whimsical curiosity."

Rish barked a laugh. "To think, I considered you the best match for my son."

"Your eldest son. You have others, and yeah, I am. You don't want to throw any other women at him. My dragon will not take it well."

Rish snickered. "I have a few ladies that I would like to sic her on."

"I am sure, but nothing is going to keep her from her mate. She mutters about it every time she sees him." Trin stretched out her bare feet and wiggled her toes.

"Is she settling at all?"

"A bit. The flights are helping."

"How is the obfuscation coming?"

"The light bending? It is great. I can fly over other cities, and none of their defenses are triggered." She chuckled. "I can even do it while human if I try really hard."

Rish sat up straighter than normal. "Really?"

Trin held up her teacup and made her hand invisible. "The only problem is that it only works on my skin, and public nudity is not acceptable."

Rish blinked. "Ah. I understand."

"It seems to be linked to the dragon energy that is seeping into my skin."

"Is it hardening your skin?"

Trin shook her head. "No, but it is in my muscles, tendons, and bones. Oh, and my nails can now carve stone."

Rish held up her hand in a gesture of restraint. "I will take your word on it. That table is an antique."

Chuckling, Trin finished her tea with a nice and normally visible hand. "Are we going to continue?"

"No, I think we are done for the day." Rish touched her jaw gingerly.

"Just a quick question. Did you travel when you were a hunter?"

"I am still a hunter, I just travel less." Rish smiled. "Being with the ones we love makes us more valuable to our homes over time, and we have to accept that."

Trin made a face. "I like being able to be where I need to be."

Rish was wistful. "My life used to be like that. I had Brommin, and things changed. Some changes were good, and others were restrictive. I had to pick my battles, and fighting for Makros's political gain was my choice."

"Well, I am going to take every chance I can to get out of the city and do some travelling. I really miss it."

"Oh, did you travel?"

"Yeah. I sourced all the products and suppliers for the first shops. Everything was handpicked by me." She felt the pride welling up in her. She and Brenner had worked hard, and their current success was a testament to that.

Rish nodded. "Good. If you ever need to travel for council business, it is an excellent thing that you have experience with it."

She shrugged. "I have travelled on my own up and down the coastline as well as into the southern interior. Coffee and tea don't go wandering on their own, you have to head out to find them."

"Do you have your own karros?"

"No. I rode a velocipede."

Rish's amazement was in her face. "Those things are deadly."

"Only if you fall off." Trin grinned. "I only ditched it once."

"What happened?" Her tutor was fascinated.

"I ended up using my travel insurance. Two weeks and seventy-three stitches later and I was back on my way."

"What kind of a vehicle was it?"

"Enfield with the wide tires. Exposed

gearing chains."

"Do you have scarring?"

Trin snorted. "No. That should have been an indicator. I never thought to ask why the marks had completely disappeared."

Rish blinked slowly. "What?"

"I don't keep scars. My body keeps healing. Isn't that a dragon thing?"

Rish shook her head. "No. No, it isn't. That is unique to you. Did they take blood from you when you arrived?"

"They did. I am sure that the alchemist is in her lab, working on figuring out what makes me tick."

"Right. I am sure of it." She didn't look happy about it.

Trin smiled. It appeared that Makros was keeping secrets from his wife.

"Well, I suppose that we should

break for lunch. You are going to have your hands full this afternoon."

"Right. I had better get changed. I am planning lunch in the commissary today, so I need to be respectable looking."

Rish gave her a sympathetic look. "Are you making friends?"

"I think so. I mean, I have plenty of friends outside of the dragon shifters, so I am not worried, but blending in is one of the skills Brommin is testing me on, so I have to behave like I belong there. So, I will."

"Are you enjoying the training? I mean, it isn't something that you were expecting."

Trin rubbed the back of her neck. "I wasn't expecting anything. I just wanted to go to work, fix the antique equipment, and focus on the controlled expansion of our shops. That was my life plan. Making a plan for courtships and mating is left to the shifters in these cities." She tapped the tattoo at the base of her neck. "I, as you can plainly see, am a human."

Rish snorted. "We can have that removed if you like."

"No. It is part of me. I have worn it for over a decade. I wouldn't know who I was without it." She patted it softly and then got to her feet. "Now, I have to be someone pleasant in normal and respectable clothing. See you tomorrow?"

"I think we can take a day off. My ears are still ringing." Rish got to her feet.

They headed for the changing area and helped the other to get back into their skirts and corsets. The workout gear was set aside for laundering, and they parted ways, leaving the sub-basement for their own personal agendas. Trin was unsurprised to see Rish heading for the senator's private offices. It was a domestic situation that didn't need to be seen to be understood. Orisha was after information, and she was very good at hitting her target. Trin almost pitied the most powerful man in the city.

She smiled to herself and headed up to the dining area. She was working at blending in, but the moment that she walked into the space with her signature white hair, all conversation stopped.

Trin settled for standing out, and she cruised through the crowds easily, finding the station that had the food she wanted. Pasta, a salad, and a side of roast in gravy were just what she wanted.

She sashayed around the room until she got a small booth to call her own, and then, she smiled and nodded for tea when the server came around.

Eating neatly in public was an art form. She practiced and was fine with the occasional glances and whispers that were thrown her way. When she was getting ready to set her utensils aside, she tensed when a dining partner slid into the seat across from hers.

"Miss Lem, I do hope that I am not interrupting you." Torm, her grabby and ex-guard smiled brightly at her.

She leaned back as the server came by and whisked away her plates. "It is no interruption, but I thought you were in some kind of program for males with poor impulse control."

His smile took on a strange twist. "I was. I have been declared to be cured of my mania."

"Excellent and congratulations." She took a sip of her tea.

He began to eat his meal. "So, I was wondering what it would take to get you to put me on your list in case Brommin is taken by the time you are allowed your choice."

"You believe that I won't get there in time?"

"Your punctuality at the annual gathering is not in question. Your social standing will determine your position in the choosing. Currently, your position is determined by your family, and that is not a particularly useful connection as you don't have one."

Trin nodded. Apparently, her connection to one of the lords wasn't well known. Good, her secrets were hers until she needed to share them. She had used that technique in the past, and there was no time like the present.

It took a lot of concentration, and she used all of her recently learned skills, but she kept herself polite and interested to Torm's conversation until she could ease herself out of the booth for her appointment.

If Brommin didn't give her a high mark for her performance at lunch, she was going to let her dragon braid his hair. It was a weird fantasy that her inner beast had, but if he gave her any lip, she was setting her crystal inhabitant loose on him with some ribbons and a hairbrush.

Chapter Two

Trin stood in a room that was dimly lit. The light flashed on for a moment and then went dark.

"Gather a scroll, the flashlight, a pen, and a feather." Brommin's selections were as arbitrary as ever.

She moved easily through the darkness and got the items that he mentioned without touching anything else. The feather was in the vase on the mantlepiece, so she lifted it out with care and precision. Trin retreated to the entry point, and she opened the door carefully, flicking from dragon eyes to human at the moment she turned the door handle.

Brommin glanced at his watch. "Well done, and no sign of your dragon. Excellent."

Trin clapped her hands around her found objects. "What is next?"

"Nothing. You have an afternoon off. What are you going to do with it?"

Trin looked him over, smiled, and sighed. "I am going to visit my god-daughter. I have to meet Brenner this evening to check out the location of a new site."

Brommin took the items from her and set them aside. "You are going to open a new shop?"

"Eventually. I believe the building needs some upgrades before we can set it up." She grimaced. "The joys of being a small-business owner."

He looked her over and paused. "Do you have a steak knife under your sleeve?"

She turned her wrist up and looked at the subtle outline that showed under the fabric. "Yes. Yes, I do."

"Why?"

"I had a lunch companion that I didn't trust. This was in case he got grabby again."

Brommin tensed. "Torm is out?"

"Yes. He joined me in the commissary. I remained pleasant and polite just in case it was a test."

"What did he say to you?"

She grimaced. "He said that my dragon will pick last and I should put him on my list in case you were taken when I get to choose."

Brommin's complexion darkened suddenly. "He said what?"

"He said—"

Brommin held up his hand. "I heard you."

He stepped in and took her hands. "I don't care if I have to hide from every woman at the ball, I will wait for you."

Trin blinked and looked up at him. Her dragon was getting to her feet and ruffling her wings.

Brommin leaned in and gave her a polite kiss with his fingers tense around hers. They were both holding back.

She lifted up on her toes and let the energy of the slight contact move through her. Her beast was on its own hind legs in her mind, enjoying the scent of her mate as his body took on the waves of heat that she was looking for.

Trin slowly lowered herself back to flat feet before things got out of control. The skin of her torso was pressing against her corset in a rapid rhythm. Her breasts were doing their best to heave behind their confines of cambric, steel, and the heavy weight of her dress.

Brommin's eyes were heavy-lidded, his skin was flushed, and there was a strange tightness over his cheekbones. He had gone from being aggressively attractive to looking predatory in those few moments. Trin's dragon made happy noises at her ability to have that effect on her mate.

Brommin drew in a slow breath through his nose, nostrils flaring. "That was... I didn't expect that response from him."

Trin blushed and shifted back a few

inches. "I am less surprised. She has been very forward when it regards you."

"What is your opinion on the matter?" He reached out and cupped her jaw.

Trin wrapped her hand around his wrist. "Like I have said before, I never planned this, but if you are willing to deal with me and my place in the world, I am willing to deal with yours."

"A dragon with your ties to the outside world hasn't been seen before. I am looking forward to what happens next. The archives are waiting eagerly."

His thumb was stroking her cheek, and she reluctantly pulled his hand away. "I am sorry. I have a meeting in an hour and another meeting after that."

His smile was wryly amused.

"Should I be getting used to this?"

"Yes. It would be best. Of course, once you and I are official, you can come with me without raising eyebrows."

Brommin shook his head. "It is strange that you are authorized to move around without an escort, but since that is what my father has decided, I wish you only the safest of freedoms."

Trin snorted. "So, you are not a fan of my running around on my own?"

"No, but unless I am part of your detail, I am not allowed to accompany you. That is not exactly making me happy right now."

She gave him a small smile. "As long as Torm keeps his distance, I am in no danger."

"He will, or he will be missing a limb

during the grand ball."

Brommin's dark expression didn't leave her guessing at which limb he was referring to.

She inclined her head and smiled tightly. "Don't worry. He makes her irritated and nauseous at first sight. That is never a good thing."

Brommin smiled slightly. "That makes me feel better."

She chuckled. "I thought it might. See me out?"

He offered her his arm, and they walked from the testing area, through shelves of ancient tomes, and finally to the lift.

Trin walked into the lift with a spring in her step. She turned and waved at Brommin before the doors closed. She quickly jabbed the button for the upper floor before the doors reopened. That would have been embarrassing.

She was sure that she had a grin on her face when she picked up her communicator and called Creata's home.

The maid at the Tal residence was a blockade. "Madam is not available."

"Well, if she is but is dodging calls, let her know that she has three minutes to call me if she wants a pastry from Miiko's."

"Miss Lem?" The maid was suddenly broadcasting relief.

"Yes, Tolla."

"Please, come by and bring the missus whatever you can to help her mood. She is very dark right now."

"I am on my way. Make sure she has a shower."

"She won't listen to me, Miss Lem."

"Give it a try. Expect me within the hour."

Tolla let out a relieved sigh. "I will have tea ready. Thank you, Miss Lem."

Trin hung up and grabbed her coat. She had a bakery to raid before she made her appearance at the Tal household. This sounded serious.

She walked up to the Tal mansion with a stack of bakery boxes dangling from her fingers. Miiko's was always a good place to strike if you were a regular. When Telber learned that it was for Creata, he had made up several of her favourites in a few minutes. He wished the new mother nothing but the best.

Trin walked up to the double doors and smiled as they were opened for her at precisely the right time.

The feeling of the house was different than it had been at the weekend. There was a depression that was hanging over the space that Trin wanted to get to the bottom of.

Vasic was out of town, and as she handed the boxes to Tolla, Trin jerked her head toward the stairs that led to the bedrooms.

"I am heading up there. Don't do anything until I call for tea. When I do, we will have it outside on the patio."

Tolla and the other maid nodded.

With her shoulders straight, Trin headed up the stairs into the literal lion's den.

Trin didn't knock, she opened the door to the master bedroom and walked in, waving her fingers at the new baby before approaching the bed where Creata was hiding.

She reached out and yanked the covers away, unsurprised when a lioness was curled where the woman should be.

"Knock it off, Creata. Your family needs you, your household needs you, and your bedding needs changing. Get up."

Creata lunged at her, teeth exposed and claws out.

Trin moved between her and the baby, using her dragon to give her the strength she needed to hold her friend at bay while the lioness attacked.

Her clothing surprisingly stood up to the clawing, and when she had Creata pinned to the floor, her friend emerged from the fur and claws.

"Oh god, Trin, I didn't mean to hurt you."

"It's fine, Creata. Now, get up and have a shower. You deserve to smell clean. I am taking the baby down to the garden. Come on down when you are done. I went to Miiko's. I got some treats for you."

She helped her naked friend to her feet and eased her into the en suite until Creata was standing in front of the shower. Trin ran the water and then triggered the spray. Creata stepped into the spray, and she started to sob.

Trin rubbed her friend's back while she used the water to hide her tears. It took several minutes for the wave of sobs to stop, but when Creata finished, she looked at Trin with a watery smile. "I think I am going to wash my hair now. I am good. I will see you downstairs in ten."

Trin nodded. "I will see you in the garden. It is a glorious day, and the baby looks like she can use some fresh air."

Trin checked in the mirror, and Creata was indeed shampooing her hair.

She scooped up the baby, who was sweet-smelling and happy. At least the baby was getting attention from her mom. It was one bit of relief in the situation.

Trin headed downstairs with the little one in her arms, and she nodded to Tolla. "Her bed needs a cleaning, and the mattress needs airing."

"Is madam well?"

"She is not well, and she and I will discuss that, but for now, she needs clean bedclothes, and the mattress needs to be taken care of. We are going to have tea in the garden."

The baby squirmed against her shoulder.

"Would you like some water and bandages?"

Trin looked at the blood on her hands. "After the bedroom is taken care of."

"Yes, Miss Trin." Tolla smiled and bowed before heading upstairs.

Amesthet chuckled and waved her fists as Trin carried her into the bright light of the early afternoon.

"So, little miss, has your mom been under the weather?"

The small gurgle that emerged was noncommittal.

Trin played with the baby for six minutes, and then, she smiled as Creata came out of the house, damp but smiling.

The smile was on Creata's lips, but her eyes were dark. Trin sighed. This was going to be a long visit.

Chapter Three

It took three hours, two feedings for the little princess, and nine of the pastries before Creata was willing to admit that she had a problem.

"I don't know what to do, Trin. Without Vasic here, I am completely lost." Creata was holding the baby and playing with one of her chubby little hands.

"Will you take some advice?"

Creata sniffed. "You don't know what it's like. You don't have a child."

"Not yet, but I do know that I take help when it is offered to me." Trin looked at her friend calmly.

Creata blinked and blushed. "I am so sorry. I don't know why I said that."

"I know that you don't. That is why I have a name and a number for you. She will even come to the house."

Creata blinked. "She?"

"I have an acquaintance who is a counsellor, and she can help you work through this time. She can also set you up with a companion to help you through until your body stops grieving for the pregnancy. It shouldn't grieve, it was a success, but it is flooding you with chemicals that make you over analyze everything until you can barely move. You aren't too far along though. You are still taking care of her, and that means you are fighting through."

Creata gave her a long look and then

asked, "Can you make the call?"

"I will, but you will speak to her. Her name is Jiirel Makintosh, and she will be able to help you work through this, even getting you to your doctor when you need it. Okay?"

"Okay."

Trin brought out her com and punched in the number.

"You have it memorized?" Creata swallowed.

"I do. You know me and numbers. Okay. Hello, Jiirel, I have someone who wishes to talk to you."

She handed over her com and took the baby from Creata, wiping the drool from her face and stroking her chubby cheek.

Trin looked up when her com was slid across the table.

"Thank you, Trin. She will be here in an hour."

Trin looked at the determined hope in her friend's eyes. "Excellent. In that case, I had better be on my way. I have an appointment with Brenner and Ni-ida. We need to discuss the new shop, and that has to be done in person."

Creata's eyes welled with tears. "Right. You have your life."

"You have a life as well. You have volunteering, charities, the baby, your hobbies, and friends who love you. You are on a new path now, but it doesn't mean that it is a bad one. You just have to get used to it. Change is hard. Welcoming it is torture." Trin stood up and pressed a kiss to her friend's forehead.

Creata chuckled. "I keep forgetting."

"Wanna know a secret?" Trin

grinned. "Me too."

"How are you adapting to it?"

Trin sighed and straightened her skirts, checking for the weapons she had cached under her corset and on her thighs. "I think I am doing well. They are keeping me busy and not restricting me as much as they were. It is something I have to get used to, but keeping in touch with the things that make me feel normal is vital. You and the baby, Brenner and Niida, the shops and everything in them helps me to lock onto reality and hold on tight when I spin out of control."

"How are the slashes on your arm?"

Trin pulled back her sleeves and showed the pale pink marks on her arms. "I heal really quick now. In a few hours, there won't be any marks at all."

Creata grabbed her arm. "Do you know how unusual that is?"

Looking at her expression, Trin caught on. "I am guessing that it is really rare."

"We can't heal like that unless we shift, and no one alerted me to a dragon in the garden."

Creata's face was serious, and Trin was relieved. This was her studious friend, and it was the first time she had seen her all day.

Trin gave her a sly look. "Can you look into it?"

Creata blinked and then nodded. "I can. Now go. Don't want you to miss your meeting. Amesthet needs toys for the holidays, and I need more pastries."

"I live to serve my adorable over-lords." Trin laughed. "I will talk to you tomorrow."

"Thanks, Trin. I mean it." Creata gave her a sober look. "Thanks."

With one final nod of acknowledgment, she left her friend and the baby and headed off to her meeting. The day had to get better.

The sun was setting, and the air was cool. Trin thought about Creata's current state during her entire forty-five-minute walk. She caught more than her fair share of stares walking alone as dark came on, but she was armed, irritated, and in clothing that would shift with her. They could try something if they wanted to pull back a stump.

The streets were quiet, in the lull of the dinner hour. The architecture was the same as it had been two centuries earlier. Three-story structures with glass-paned storefronts, apartments above each, lined the street in a variety of stone. Limestone, sandstone, and even some well-worn soapstone. Granite was reserved for the more upscale neighbourhoods.

Looking around at Forest Avenue, she saw just what her research had shown her. This neighbourhood needed a coffee and a tea shop. The street catered to working couples of every shifter clan and a lot of mixed groupings. They needed a place to get coffee, tea, and pastries. If the shops could grow over the next year, they would be on board for the next phase of the Harbinger line. Harbinger Snacks.

The snack shop would bring in a line of themed food from around the world and offer them for sale from five in the morning until one in the afternoon. With enough demand, they would have their snacks going until seven in the evening. That would require double the staff and heavy overtime. The spine of sales had to be firm before they risked anything like that.

She analyzed the side-by-side door-ways at the address, and she nodded. They weren't ideal, but she could work with them.

Trin stepped into the building, and as she turned to lock up behind her, she saw the same vehicle that had gone around the block three times while she was walking along. That wasn't suspicious at all.

"Trin! Is that you?"

Trin grinned and headed toward

Brenner's voice. "It is. What is your general impression of this place?"

Brenner was standing with his arms around his wife. Niida looked tired.

She smiled at the couple and looked around at the rich wood and polished stone. "I think that this is an ideal location. I have seen nine operating businesses on this block alone, and none are competitors."

Brenner grinned. "Good. The paperwork is on the table. We are just going to stand here and enjoy being still."

Trin nodded and did her checks. The building was divided, but a door through the connecting wall was possible as long as they got the correct permits. The ability to get the permits was a condition of the sale.

Inside the restrooms, she found the

plumbing working as advertised, a few tiles needed to be replaced, but she was planning a renovation. The contractor and designer worked well together, which was fortunate, as they were a couple.

Trin checked the space in the area that would become the kitchen. It had enough room and more than enough grounded electrical hookups. It was good to go.

She returned to the front of the shop and smiled at Brenner. "I am willing to sign the purchase offer if you are."

He nodded. "You know that the other building has had a fire."

"Yeah, I have put that into our numbers. I will just check the caveats in the contract, and you two can get a good night's sleep."

Niida chuckled. "That would be a blessing. My morning sickness has kicked in, and the only time I am not ill is when I am at work."

Trin made a commiserating sound and rubbed her shoulder. "It will be over soon. By this time next year, your baby will be crawling around on the floor and will be going over to Creata's for play dates."

Brenner chuckled and rested his chin on Niida's head. "That is what I told her, but I don't have your delivery."

Trin flipped an empty bucket over and went through all the details of the contract, flagging and making changes as she went along. If the seller didn't agree to the changes in the contract, Trin and Brenner had other sites on their radar.

She signed her name with a flourish. It was the only time she used the whole thing. Adolla Valtrin Lem was quite the awkward signature.

Trin handed the mass to Brenner and nodded. "Go over it. I can take over holding Niida if need be."

Niida chuckled and stepped away from her husband. "I am fine. His scent just soothes me."

"Understandable."

Brenner took the pages and looked at all the red marks she had made. "This is going to take a while."

Trin nodded. "Yeah. This was not a great contract. Our initial offer was lost in their counteroffers. The changes I want to make won't cost much but will save us time."

Niida smiled. "Would you like to see

the apartments?"

"Sure. Or, maybe I could scan the other side. We want a complete gut job for our scent-dampening installation. I would like to estimate removal costs."

Brenner waved at her. "Go ahead, ladies. I thought my days of doing homework were over."

His wife gave him a kiss, and then, both women walked out the back door and entered the second building.

The smell of a bonfire was everywhere. Niida wrinkled her nose and inhaled deeply. "I can handle this."

"Good." Trin stepped deeper into the building and kept an eye on the strength of the floor. She didn't want to face Brenner if Niida dropped into the basement.

"So, Trin, do you enjoy living with

the dragons?"

Trin grinned and thumped a post, watching the ash rain down. "I enjoy it on a certain level. Learning to be a dragon has been weird."

"Well, good or bad weird?"

"Mostly good. The women are angry, and the men are predatory. It keeps me on my toes."

She looked around and saw that this interior was larger than the other side. It wasn't an illusion, it was a genuinely huge room.

"I think Brenner is going to have to talk to the designer and the contractor. This place will definitely be larger than the other side when finished."

"Really? That's great. By the way, do you have a male you are interested in?"

Trin glanced back at the innocent

look illuminated by the glow of the phones in their hands. "My dragon has picked one. I must confess that it is rather nice that I don't have to involve myself in the process. It has been a lot easier to see her choice and look for his better qualities. He has a lot of them."

"Is it Brommin?"

"It is. So, Brenner has told you that much."

"Two of his sisters come by the shop during the day, and they gossip about you incessantly. They are both impressed and intimidated. It is a suitable reaction in my experience."

Trin laughed and continued to work at checking the building for damage.

Twenty minutes kicking and pulling at the timbers and she was sure. This place would be great. They had parking, a back garden that could be coaxed to life, and plenty of space to host the shops.

"Let's head back to see how Brenner is doing."

They went through the front door, and Niida had just walked into the first side they had visited when a vehicle cruised past on the road. The sound of the pulse gun was unmistakable. The blast caught Trin in the ribs and threw her back into the stone front of the building.

The vehicle roared off, but Trin knew who it was as she lay on the ground, getting her breath back and checking for damage to her corset.

Brenner rushed out, and Niida was dialling frantically.

Trin grunted as Brenner moved her to

get her inside. "Who are you calling?"

"Brommin. He said that if anything ever happened to you, to call."

Trin smelled blood from the crack to the back of her head against the stone, and she pressed her hand to her scalp. "Aw, fuck."

She sat with her friends and felt the soreness in her abdomen fade with every passing second. *I am working to heal you quickly, but it would be easier if I had my mate.*

Trin sighed and spoke to her dragon. *There is a special event for that. You will have him soon.*

The delight in her dragon when the heavy beat of wings sounded in the street was unmistakable. The prized and desired dragon in question had arrived.

<h1 style="text-align:center">Chapter Four</h1>

$\mathcal{B}$rommin's dragon feet had barely touched the ground when he was shifted and walking toward the shop.

He was dressed in black from head to toe, and it looked amazing on him.

"Trin, what is wrong? What did they hit you with?"

She wrinkled her nose as he examined her scorched clothing. "Pulse gun."

He froze. "You should be dead."

"I know. My dragon wasn't convinced. She thought I could take the hit. I wasn't counting on striking the façade of the building." She touched her head.

The blood was gone, and there was only a slightly sensitive spot where it had been.

She smiled at his worried face. "I am fine. She took care of the repairs."

Brommin scowled and investigated the back of her head. There was dried blood on her scalp, and she could feel his hands tense. "You could have split your skull."

"I didn't do it. The blast did it."

Brenner and Niida were standing next to each other. Brenner cleared his throat. "She was thrown back at least twelve feet. I thought she was dead until she sat up and cursed."

Trin was surrounded by folks who wanted her to be alive and well. "I am fine. I even have the plate number of the vehicle that struck me, and a description of the man who shot the plasma rifle."

Brommin nodded. "You are coming back to the tower. We will get to the bottom of this and find out what is what."

Niida cleared her throat. "They were behaving as if there was a contract out on Trin. They stalked her and made sure she was here on this street when they struck."

Trin looked at her. Niida had untapped skills.

Niida shrugged. "I noticed that they circled at least three times while you were on your way here. That isn't normal. This area is tucked in after dark."

Trin blushed while Brommin ran his hands over her torso. "I don't think your mother would approve."

He looked up at her, and a slow smile spread over his lips. "I am fairly sure she would. She is a great fan of yours."

Trin put her hands over Brommin's and smiled slightly. "I don't think she would enjoy a public display."

"Ah. Right. You are probably correct." He winked. "You don't seem damaged, which is rather surprising. Even for you."

She chuckled. "My dragon is doing what it can to fix everything, but my head is still a little sore."

He nodded and turned his hands to grip hers as he rose to his feet. She came with him.

"I am going to make a few calls, and then, we will make a plan. Do you feel that this place is safe?"

Niida nodded. "I thought she was dead, so I am pretty sure those who pulled the trigger did, also."

Brommin's hands tightened on Trin's. "I am going to make those calls."

He took out his communicator and wandered to the rear of the building, speaking softly the moment he got a connection.

Trin looked at Brenner. "Sorry about this."

The curse that exploded from Niida was enough to take them both aback. When she calmed, she said, "This is not your fault, Trin. Nothing is your fault. You have been dealt a very weird hand, and you are coping."

Trin grinned. "Thanks, Niida. I needed that."

Her friend stepped forward and gave her a hug. Brenner followed suit.

Trin chuckled and returned the embrace. "This is going on record as being the weirdest season ever."

Brenner murmured, "You really have it bad for Brommin."

"How can you tell?"

He chuckled and leaned back. "You didn't punch him when he grabbed your waist."

"Oh, yeah. That. I may have accepted it as concern for me." Trin smiled.

"A weird season, indeed." Niida giggled.

Brommin was pacing, and his free hand was clenching. He was not in a calm mood.

Trin murmured to Brenner, "I think I might want to take a trip to source out some new herbal teas, coffees, and crockery."

"I think that is a great idea. Does Mirbella still have your go-bag?"

"Yup. I am sure that I can deal with the assassination attempts, but without knowing who is behind it, things could continue." She grimaced. "I don't know how long I want to be on guard, and I would hate it for my father to be the culprit."

Brenner shook his head. "I still can't believe that he was able to breed outside of the mating."

Trin blinked in mock horror, "Maybe he didn't, and you have imagined me all along."

Niida snorted.

Brommin came back, his jaw tense and shoulders tight. "It is official. There is a price on your head. Death is the only option, and the contract has been spread through every assassin society in the city. We are going to have to hide you."

Trin smiled. "How about I just make myself scarce?"

"What?"

"I have some business to attend to in a few cities. I can call you to check in, and you can look for the idiot who wants me dead."

He gave her a look that said she wasn't too bright. "There will be stories if a crystal dragon is known to be travelling the coast and interior."

Trin took his hand and held it. "Unlike most dragons, I am not used to flying when I travel. I have a route, folks know me, and I won't stray too far from my normal path and safety net. I can do what needs to be done and touch base with my sources, and you can seek and destroy my enemies here."

He blinked and looked down at her grip on his hand. He flexed his fingers, and their hands wound together. "If you agree to call once a day, every day. Even just one word and I will know that you are fine."

"Done. I will just get my vehicle from Creata's, and I will be on my way." She didn't mention that she was stopping at Mirbella's to get her clothing and travel documents.

"Good. Call me at exactly this time tomorrow, or I will find you." He leaned in and pressed a kiss to her lips.

Her dragon was eager to have him, but she was also eager to see the world, even through Trin's eyes. She was on board, no matter what a velocipede was, the dragon was willing to find out.

Trin wrapped her hand around his

neck and held on tight as she worked to remember the taste of him. It was Brenner clearing his throat that finally got her attention and made her back off.

She felt her lips humming, and there was that predatory look in Brommin's eyes that she so enjoyed. "Right. I am guessing that I should be off."

Niida was grinning. "Everybody has been notified. Get your velocipede and go. I look forward to the new crockery, china, and teas."

Brenner put his arm around his wife. "Did you want a ride to Creata's?"

Brommin shook his head. "I will take her. When I lift you, look limp. I want anyone spying to think that you are injured at the very least."

Trin nodded. "I can play dead. Are we going now?"

Brommin nodded. "We are."

He didn't give her a chance to say goodbye, simply lifted her into his arms and left the shop, heading to the street.

Trin let her arm hang and whispered to Brenner, "Let me know if they fall for the offer."

He laughed just as quietly, and then, Niida whispered, "Good luck and stay safe."

Trin fought her smile as Brommin flexed his wings and she kept herself floppy and loose as he bent and launched them upward.

"So, do you have any other conditions to impose on me while I travel?"

He looked down at her, and his face was being kept grim with effort she could see. "I want you safe, and I want you to promise to let your dragon out when she demands it. She will be able to keep you safe."

"Got it. In case of emergency, break cover."

"Vasic also has a file for you with all the details of your mother's family, if that happens to be near one of your routes."

She blinked. "That was not on my list."

"It is your first assignment. You can get in and out legally, looking for your parents. Few can get in and out of that valley."

Trin didn't nod, but she knew about the settlements versus the cities. She had access to a few settlements but getting in was always an effort. They didn't want any plants, animals, or technology that wasn't already in use in their agrarian areas. They defended their farms to the death. It made visiting the settlements rather tricky.

His wings carried them over the city, and her lolling head saw the Tal residence. He brought them down in the backyard, and Creata was waiting for them.

Creata cried out and ran toward them, but Trin lifted her head and smiled. "I am fine. Just a bit dented."

Brommin set her on her feet, and she hugged Creata the moment that her friend stumbled into her arms.

"I am sorry for the scare, Creata. You don't deserve any other stress."

Creata stiffened her spine and nodded. "You don't deserve to be shot, but you were. Vasic is coming home, so this is the perfect time for Ystine to leave the shed."

Brommin's voice was curious. "Ystine?"

Trin was still holding Creata. "My velo. We built it together when I needed to travel. It was cheaper than having me on mass transport, and I found the experience exhilarating. Ystine is a true group effort."

"I look forward to meeting her."

Creata chuckled. "She will be looking forward to meeting you."

Creata pushed away and wiped her eyes. "I have been tweaking her a little. She is ready to travel."

Trin blinked and slowly grinned. "This I have got to see."

Creata took her hand and led the way to the rear of the huge garden, through some trees, and to a workshop painted to look like the brush around them.

"I didn't know that you had put such effort into it."

Creata smiled. "Vasic thinks that I like the gardens. I had a scrubber put in so that I always come out smelling the same way I went in. The boiler suit was stretched to capacity when I was pregnant, but it gave me something to do when Vasic was out of town."

Creata pressed her palm to the lock and the heat and pressure of her hand set the gears and tumblers in motion. The wide doors slid aside, and in the center of a polished concrete space was Trin's travel companion.

"Ah, Ystine, you look wonderful."

Lights sparked on the edge of the handlebars. "Thank you, Trin. You are looking well, also. Have you been recently injured?"

A beam of light shot over Trin. "You have been hit with a blast to the chest, and your skull was cracked but is healing at a rapid pace. Congratulations on your evolution."

Trin walked over and asked, "May I touch you?"

"Of course. You are my rider. No one else may touch me."

Bronze, steel, gears, panels of polished wood, small indicator lights, and a new attachment. "Is this a screen?"

"Of course. It isn't safe for you to check your com and drive. It is a complete com panel with navigation." Creata stepped forward and asked for Ystine's permission before she began to flick through the options. "They are all on voice request as well."

Trin glanced back, and Brommin was staring at them as if they had suddenly transformed. "You look confused, Brommin."

"This is not what I had envisioned as a hobby for Creata. Does Vasic know?"

Creata chuckled. "I told him that I come here to make things if that makes it better. He has just never asked what it is that I make."

Brommin blinked. "You look so... sweet."

Trin looked at Creata and giggled. She was wearing a frilly nightgown covered by a frillier robe. She looked adorable and feminine, soft as a flower petal, but that overlooked the stems and thorns she had grown when her family had refused to claim her.

Creata raised her eyebrows. "I deceive folks by simply being what I am and doing what I can do to keep myself busy. It was holding back that caused a bit of the difficulty I have been finding myself in. From now on, I am going to do what I need to do, and I will teach the baby to do it from the time she can walk. Vasic can do his work for the senate; I will do what I need to here, as long as I need to do it."

Trin stroked the velo again. "Who designed your brain, Ystine?"

"Brenner was my main creator, but Creata shaped all of my systems."

"Your voice is familiar."

"Your friend Apraxa contributed my voice. You always liked listening to the sound of her speaking. You told Creata that it was like listening to the sea, so she got Apraxa to record the words for her."

Trin blinked and then grinned. "It is a voice I always listen to. It always sounds like music."

Brommin came forward and cocked his head. "Who is Apraxa?"

He carefully kept his distance from the velocipede, but he examined it from its wide tires, comfortable seat, and sloped handlebars.

Creata smiled. "Apraxa is a specialist at acquiring what is needed from something small to a ship. I have been in correspondence with her for a few years now. She is charming, even in prose."

"Is she a shifter?"

Trin shook her head. "She's a half-breed. All the lineage, none of the extra energy to shift."

Brommin cocked his head. "What is

she?"

"She's half shark." Trin smiled. "The teeth didn't translate to her born form, and she has skin like a peach."

"Shark? They are thugs, organized crime." Brommin's brow furrowed.

"And very good at moving things through customs that have gotten stuck by bureaucrats who want a bribe." She shook her head. "Dealing in tea can be a nasty game."

Creata piped up, "It is why she gets most of her product from the mainland."

Trin stopped her slow caress of the velo. "Well, if everyone is good, I am going to be on my way. It will be hard enough to get Ystine through the streets."

Creata straightened and moved to the

side of the workshop. She pulled a leaver, and the sound of gears and chains could be heard. A panel in the floor lowered until it formed a ramp leading down into darkness.

"I made a few escape routes with a tunneller. This will take you under the main streets, and Ystine can get you to the southern or northern gates, as you like." Creata paused, and tears welled in her eyes. "I am going to be counting on that ping."

"I won't leave you hanging." Trin hugged her. "Now, I have to get going, or I won't be out of flight range by dawn."

Brommin waited until she was free of her friend, and then, he took her hand and knelt. "When you return, I will ask you for your hand, but for now, will you choose me when the time comes?"

She got a little teary-eyed. "Always. I choose you now, and I choose you then."

He grinned and placed a soft kiss on the palm of her hand. "Be safe and stay clear of the city until I assure you it is safe or for the ball. I really want you there at that ball."

He pressed his forehead to hers, and she felt the rumble of his dragon speaking to the strident tones of hers. They stayed like that for several moments, and when the dragons had completed their conversation, Trin pulled back, got on Ystine, pulled her skirts into a stable position, and she started the deep purr of her velocipede.

She didn't look back, merely pulled her helmet from the attachment spot on the side of her transport and throttled forward, into the dark. Time to ride.

Chapter Five

Ystine's lights came on automatically, and she asked, "Would you like me to plot a course through the tunnels?"

"Please. I have a pretty good idea where we are going, but I am not sure of landmarks."

"There aren't any. Creata told me while she was working on me that no one would be able to find their way out without the map. She gave me the map." Ystine's voice was low and cheerful, coming in through the headset in the helmet.

"She is good at maps and puzzles. I

am guessing that this is one of them."

Ystine paused and then asked, "Should we not mention that you are no longer human?"

"I am still partially human, I have just had the other portion activated. Please lock that in your databanks. It is sensitive information that could get me killed in the wrong location."

"Filing the sensitivity away. It will remain locked in my databanks so that I recognize you, but no one else will gain that information."

"Thank you." She knew that Ystine would have picked up on her change in energy pattern. They were in direct contact in at least three places, after all.

They rode in silence for three turns, and then, Ystine announced, "We are under the dress shop. There is a compressed ladder under the seat."

Trin dismounted and smiled at the balance that Ystine had on her own. Wide tires rocked.

She was just flipping up the seat when a hatch opened ten feet above her, and a rope and wood ladder tumbled down, missing her by inches.

"That works as well." She removed her helmet and left it with Ystine.

Trin pulled the ladder tight and started to climb. She pulled herself up into the storeroom, and Mirbella was sitting nearby with a tea service and a stack of sandwiches.

"There are more sandwiches in your pack. I must say, I never thought we would be doing this again." Mirbella smiled and poured the tea.

"It wasn't looming high on my to-do

list either, but here we are." Getting off the ladder without stepping on the half-dozen yards of fabric that made up her skirt was impossible. Trin flopped to the side when she was at hip-height and rolled to her feet.

Mirbella handed her a soft wipe for her hands and gestured for her to sit on the arranged boxes. "Now, I have a list of things for you to keep an eye out for during your travels. If you find them, I will pay just about anything for them."

"What are they?"

"Mostly buttons and clasps of certain metallic compositions. They are easier to enchant."

Mirbella's position as an actual magic user was something that was understood and not spoken about. Trin knew she liked certain metallic compositions from previous journeys, but she wasn't sure why until now.

"So even the buttons are enchanted?" She picked up her teacup and took a long sip. She didn't mind the scalding heat, she needed tea.

Mirbella smiled. "They have to be, or when you change back to your human form, the clothing would fit but flap open."

"Right. Thanks for getting this together for me."

"It is rather fun. Now, I have to make you look human without sacrificing style and the alteration-ability of the clothing. I do so love a challenge." Mirbella grinned. "I have created a leather trench coat for you, your standard trousers, an array of small weaponry, and boots suitable for use on your velocipede."

"I can't use weapons in a lot of the places I travel."

"I know. These all double as cutlery." Mirbella laughed. "I have travelled a time or two, and the worst thing you will face is a discussion on why your clothing is enchanted. You can just say it is a gift from a lover."

Trin blushed and finished her tea. "How much do I owe you?"

"Nothing for the storage of your go-bag, and I will settle the clothing with your account when you return. If you have anything for me, it will decrease your balance considerably." Mirbella winked.

"I will keep careful track." She took a sandwich and then another.

"When do you think you will be

back?"

"Before the dragon ball. I have to be there to sweep Brommin of his feet."

Mirbella nodded. "I will have something stunning ready for you. It will be something worthy of a crystal dragon. There hasn't been one of you found for over a century, at least."

"That is what they tell me, but she just sniffs when I tell her that."

Mirbella chuckled. "Dragons are noted for their disdain for the classifications of man."

"We are just a taller and bulkier form of shapeshifter."

"And you have a longer lifespan. Those who rule as a dragon provide a long and stable rule." The seamstress chuckled. "I can just enchant textiles."

Another ten minutes of chatter and it

was time for Trin to get dressed in something a little more road worthy.

When she was finished transforming, she looked at the mirror and grinned. Tight black trousers, a soft black shirt, and brown boots were crisscrossed with laces, belts, and attachments that ranged from the practical to the deadly. The coat that she put on top hid her body and left her looking like a medium-height man at first glance.

"Thank you, Mirbella. I hope to find what you are looking for."

"Drive safe, be safe, and enjoy it. Your little mission might be to protect you, but there is no saying that you can't have fun."

"I would deal with them all if I knew who they were."

Mirbella patted her shoulder. "I

know. Your homicidal rage is usually near the surface. Go. You need at least four hours of dark to get clear of the city's viewers."

"Right. Right. Wow. When this was for work, I was in a hurry, but I hate the idea that I have to run for my life."

"We all have to run when the moment comes. The true strength will be in coming home."

Trin smiled with her lips tensed. She lowered her packs through the hole in the floor and waved at Mirbella before going back down the ladder.

It was time to get down to business and escape the city.

Ystine asked her, "Which direction?"

"South. I want to get back onto the road outside the southern gate."

"We can do that."

With a final settling of her paniers, she got back on the velo. "Well, let's go."

The low rumbling purr started, and she put on her helmet. The moment that her hands hit the grips, the velocipede took off.

The headlight showed the curved walls that cupped them, and while it must have been twenty minutes of driving in the confined space, it only felt like seconds. When Ystine drove through the hidden exit, the doors flapped open as they exited and closed behind them.

A glance through the side mirror showed storm doors blending in with the shrubs around them. Damn, Creata had been busy.

The night opened up around them,

and Ystine took them south. The coast-line awaited.

Driving into the dawn brought the last seven hours to fruition. If the city was open, Trin could get what Mirbella needed and go off the grid for the rest of the trip.

She slowed Ystine and pulled over to the side of the road, lifting her visor and staring at the city at the edge of the continent.

"This view never gets old."

Ystine chuckled. "That is amusing considering that it is the second oldest city on the continent."

"Yes, but every time I see it, it has changed just enough to show growth and development but still be familiar." Trin grinned. "I like it."

"Don't you like the capital?"

"I love it, it is home, but seeing the rest of the continent makes the return to it sweeter."

"I see. Are we going to head to the city?"

"Impatient?"

"I am seeing this world for the first time. I want to see more of it."

Trin lowered her visor and got back into position. "Let's go then. Our destination is at the edge of the waterfront, Puzzletooth Avenue."

"Yes, Trin. Course is on display."

"Thanks, Ystine. Let's hope you have the current maps. The warren of roads around the waterfront is hellish."

The bike chuckled as they got underway. "I will get you through without trouble."

"This I am longing to see. Let's move." She twisted the throttle, and her velo shot forward. They had appointments to keep and trades to make. It was always a good idea to have those negotiations over breakfast.

Chapter Six

After a slow cruise through the maze of the waterfront, Trin grinned at the familiar figure lounging against the exterior of the warehouse. She pulled up next to her friend and removed her helmet.

Apraxa's gaze locked on Trin's head, and she burst out laughing. "Trin, what the hell?"

Trin reached up and stroked a hand through her hair, removing any helmet-head. "What?"

"It's white!"

"Ohh. That. Yeah. I got into an altercation with a dragon, and this was the result."

Apraxa grinned. "That sounds like a story. Are you up for breakfast?"

"I thought you would never ask. Oh, I would like to introduce you to the upgraded Ystine."

Trin set the helmet down in front of her. "Ystine, this is your voice donor, Apraxa."

"I am very pleased to meet you, Madam Tiburon."

Apraxa inclined her head formally. "I hope that you are enjoying your tone."

"It is very clear, and Trin can hear me even with the sound of the wind and road around us."

Trin smirked. "I think she just called you piercing."

Apraxa shrugged. "She isn't wrong.

If I want to, my voice can travel for miles. Now, let's get your transport with its elegant manner of speaking and tuck it away while we go for breakfast."

Trin followed Apraxa and settled Ystine inside the warehouse, placing her behind a scald shield that was cued to Trin's handprint. It was one of Apraxa's new toys.

"Where did you get this?"

Apraxa chuckled. "Creata has taken to selling her designs. She wants a nice educational fund for her child. It is a girl?"

"It is."

"Good. Creata has been a little unfocused recently. I wasn't sure that she actually knew." Apraxa led the way out of the door, locking her cavern of treasures behind her. "She is better now?"

"Since last night? Yeah. She is dealing with a few things, and I am pretty sure that her husband being out on assignment is part of it. She needs him right now."

Apraxa nodded. "My sister-in-law had similar issues. The pregnancy was hard, and her recovery was a family-wide effort. We all did our parts, and she is a mom to two more children, and everybody is aware of danger signs. There haven't been any at all this year."

"She doesn't mind that you check on her?"

"We have done it at her request. She wants us to check and let her know what we are seeing. It took a while, but now, we are all used to it."

The wind caught Apraxa's blue and crimson hair, lifting and playing with it.

Trin envied the colouring. She was stuck on the pale end of the hair spectrum.

They walked the two blocks to the seaside teashop, and though the door said *Closed*, Apraxa walked right in. Trin had been here before, so she followed.

Apraxa's three brothers were working in the shop, one out front and two behind the counter making the most exotic pastry that Trin had ever seen.

Hector, Troy, and Pollux looked up and smiled at them, their smiles turning into wide grins when they saw Trin.

She squeaked as she was hugged by the shark-shifters one by one.

Apraxa laughed and went behind the counter to grab their breakfast.

Hector set her back and looked her over. "Trin, you look wonderful. I love what you have done with your hair."

She sighed. "Thank you, Hector. How is your wife?"

He grinned wider, his telltale teeth showing. "She is wonderful, as are our three sons. Kohasi will be in later if you are still around."

"I plan on staying for two or three days."

Apraxa looked up in delight. "Really? Cool. Come on, guys, she has been travelling all night. She needs to eat."

Her host had a tray full of tea and pastries. She made her way to a table in the most comfortable part of the tea-shop. Low couches were set around a polished stone table, and Trin joined her friend at the meal of quiches, pastries, and tea so flavourful she nearly wept.

It was an excellent end to this leg of her journey and an amazing beginning to the next part of her plan.

Chapter Seven

"So, tell me why you have really made me your first stop." Apraxa walked slowly with her through the sample market and smiled at a few of the vendors.

"I need to know what you know about dragon societies, and I need some help picking out stoneware for the new shop. We are starting a line of reusable mugs."

"Nice. I think I know just the shop. Now, why do you need to know about dragons?"

"I have started seeing one, but he

isn't going to make a move because their women have to do it first, and I am not comfortable with that scenario." It was close to the truth. Apraxa was excellent at knowing things that you weren't planning on telling her.

"Wow. I thought you were going to remain single or, at least, give Pollux another chance."

"Well, I saw him, and something inside said that he was the one." Her tone was wry. It was also a truth.

"Huh. Well, yeah, the females have to make the first move, usually at a public event. If the male is a single dragon, or at least single, he really doesn't have a choice. My birth mom chose my father at a trade meeting and didn't realize he was newly married. He and his mate hadn't bonded yet. Well, that and sharks don't have breeding restrictions like the dragons do. Fidelity is not their strong suit."

"So, I have heard." Trin really wanted to ask her friend for details, but she couldn't delve into something so personal.

"I only know a bit about dragons because of my mother's family. They swam out every three months and taught me about my family and culture."

"Ah, right. Sea dragons."

"Yup. They are more laid back about social disasters than the dragons at the capital."

Trin chuckled and followed Apraxa into one of the stalls. She looked at the items on display and asked a few questions. There was a set of long-handled mugs that depicted the seasons, and they were perfect for her purposes. She requested that the colours be brighter and all of the pigments used to be safe. If she tested them and one of them was contaminated, she would return and destroy the shop. The seller was pleasant, a little nervous, but earnest. They had a deal.

With one order made, she smiled at Apraxa. "Well, one done, now we need some more delicate stuff."

"Excellent. So, I have some actual artisans that you can see. They can make what you want in a custom order."

"Right in town?"

"Right in town." They left the shop, and Apraxa casually asked, "So, why did you choose a dragon?"

Trin thought about it. "I don't know.

He just feels right in every way that matters."

"Except he is a dragon and that isn't a great situation for humans."

"Yeah, well, there is some flexibility there."

Apraxa nodded. "There is something different and yet the same about you. It is more than just the hair. What do you know about the new crystal dragon in the capital?"

"Not much. I have never seen her." That was the truth as well.

"Huh. I thought she had cruised over the city a few times."

"I work indoors. No time for looking up." Trin smiled and kept pace as they meandered out of the market and to-ward the streets of artisans.

"Are you keeping something from

me?" Apraxa asked it directly.

"I am. I can tell you in private but not walking the streets."

Apraxa nodded and then her demeanour changed. "Hang back. One of the gangs is roaming."

"Which one?"

"The Haj. Swedish bastards should never have been allowed to make their way here. They still try to pretend to be Norse, and raiding is their favourite thing."

Shouts and panicked cries emerged from one of the shops. Apraxa growled and strode forward, heading to stop the shakedown.

As silently as she had been trained to move, Trin followed. No one let a friend go into danger alone.

The shop was a teashop, which appalled Trin, but the sight of the blonde thug holding Apraxa by her neck was enough to set Trin's blood boiling.

"That is simply rude. No one should treat a lady that way."

They took in her leathers and the straps she had around her hips and thighs. One of the men laughed, "She has brought a pet human to sacrifice for the shop. How thoughtful."

The three blonde guys wearing matching clothing were too tempting. It didn't matter that they were huge. They were endangering her friend and the folk huddled in the corners. That couldn't stand.

In what felt like slow motion, she turned and kicked out at the man nearest her, sending his knee into the wrong direction. He went down, and she kept moving forward, blocking, kicking, and using pressure points until the next one was flat on his back. Now, the man holding her friend was the only one left.

"If you come closer, I break her neck. I am not joking."

She didn't comment but pulled a short blade and threw it at him, pinning his arm to the wall and forcing him to drop Apraxa.

Her friend landed on her butt and rubbed her neck as the three thugs hopped out and went to seek some medical attention.

Apraxa coughed, and the shopkeeper filled a cup and brought it over. "Thank you, Miss Tiburon, and thanks to your friend."

Trin looked around and realized that

the idiot had run off with her blade in him. She would need a replacement.

When Apraxa could speak, she sat on one of the floor cushions, and she rasped. "So, what was that?"

"Training. My fella is teaching me." Trin offered her hand to her friend. Apraxa took the hand and hauled herself to a standing position.

"He appears to be a fella with some training."

"It would seem so." She smiled politely.

The family was bowing and offering their thanks. Apraxa shook her head and smiled. "My friend here is a tea merchant in the capital. I thought of you the moment that she said she was looking for new ceramics."

The woman's eyes widened, and she

smiled. "Please, miss. Come with me and describe what you would like to have. I can show you previous pieces in our gallery, and you can let your imagination run."

Trin held up her hands. "If you are upset by the events, we can come back later."

She was grabbed by the arm and pulled along. "Nonsense. Any friend of Miss Tiburon is more than welcome, notwithstanding the assistance you gave her. That was amazing."

Trin let herself be hauled off while Apraxa spoke softly with the man and teen who had also been threatened by the thugs.

"They were shaking you down for protection money?"

The woman paused and then nodded. "It is what happens in this city. You get the trade, you get the light, and you get the sea, but you get the organizations who feel that they should get a piece of your income."

Trin decided to change the topic. "Apraxa said you are a teashop?"

"Oh, we import a few tons every year. Would you like to sample some after you look at our hardware?"

"Please." Trin smiled brightly.

They went through a door, and the scent of clay was lightly in the air. Two potters were sitting at wheels and working on teapots.

"Those are lovely, but I would like whatever design I choose to be set for mass production."

"That is easy enough. Do you have anything in mind?"

Trin nodded as they approached the display cabinet. "I am looking for something subtle and making reference to the seasons."

"Excellent."

Looking at the display, she selected a few pieces to look at, and when she had solidified an idea in her mind, she started to smile. "I think I have it."

The shopkeeper blinked. "Just like that?"

"Yes. I am fairly good at making decisions. It is part of my charm." She smiled brightly.

"Would you like to meet the artisans?"

"Please."

The next ten minutes of meeting the shopkeeper's children and their spouses took up most of her visit time. When she had introduced herself and shaken hands covered with clay and dust, she had won them over.

She was escorted to the sink where they cleaned up, and she scrubbed her hands, drying them on a towel that the potter's fifteen-year-old son had offered her. Trin knew by the look in his eyes that she had a fan.

When her host finally brought her out into the teashop, Apraxa was sitting casually on the floor next to a low table, and she was telling a very off-colour joke about a shark getting its claspers bitten off.

The weak laughter was just what she needed. "Well, Apraxa, I have made my choice. I was just about to put in the order."

The shop owner got a sketchbook and

sat with her pencil poised. "Whenever you are ready, Miss."

With a smile to the man who brought her a cup of tea, Trin got down into the details of what she was looking for. The woman got more excited, as did the folk in the shop.

Apraxa spoke softly to the men, and they immediately sprang into action, preparing a series of trays with an array of herbs and powders. They were drawing kettles of water, and Trin almost rubbed her hands together. Tea tasting was one of her favourite pastimes.

When she finished her description of what she wanted, the woman rose to her feet and left. "Huh, was it something I said?"

"No. She is going to work on the designs. Tomyo will assist us, along with

Master Gwin."

The trays of tea were being set out, the small tasting cups had the precise amount of the leaves required to bring the taste out. The master of the shop knelt across from her, and he smiled. "Thank you for coming to our shop today."

She sat up straight and inclined her head. "Thank you for receiving me."

"It is our pleasure. You are very quick."

She chuckled. "It is practice. I do not like it when folks dangle my friends."

Apraxa smiled. "I thank you for your reflexes. Did you get that dagger back?"

"My knife? No. He wore it out."

"I will get you a new one."

Trin nodded. "Thank you. Oh, any ideas where I should book a hotel while

I am here?"

"You can stay with me. I have put a house in the back of the warehouse. It is comfy, and I have a rooftop garden. Oh, and several guestrooms for the brothers when they stop by."

The tea master took the hot kettle from the younger man, and he poured water into every other cup before going back and covering the tea with a lid while it steeped.

"I would love to stay over. Now, I need to concentrate."

Apraxa held her hands up in surrender, and Trin got to work. It was time to choose some new product to keep her small empire growing.

Baby gifts and then a nap were next on the list.

Chapter Eight

The house that Apraxa had built inside her warehouse was made of scorched wood on the exterior and a bright splash of colour as soon as the door was open.

"This is impressive."

"Thank you. It took me and the guys a while to get it just right, but they are better at the interior decorating than they are at construction."

Trin chuckled. "The diner is definitely well designed."

"It really is. They are raking in tons of money for the family, and they are doing it legally. They might be invited to the New Year's Eve gathering this year." Apraxa led her into the house and up some stairs.

Light was streaming in from panels inside the walls, and it made everything inside bright and cheery.

"I can show you more after you rest, but you must be exhausted, so sleep comes first. Don't worry about Ystine, I will take care of her." Apraxa opened a door, and the guest room was exposed in all of its pale green, bamboo, and white glory. "The unit on the wall controls the light; there is an en suite to your left. I will see you when you wake up."

Trin nodded. "Thanks. I could use a few hours' rest."

Apraxa inclined her head. "I will be

working downstairs if you need anything."

With another small nod, Trin was alone. She gave herself an assessing sniff and headed toward the shower. It was important that she not contaminate her bed with the scent of the road. She might be using it a second night.

She woke up in the same dimness she had set the light to before she went to sleep. The light was slightly redder but still bright.

"Wow, she is efficient." Trin got up and grabbed her saddle bag from the end of the bed. Sometime during her nap, Apraxa had delivered her bags.

Her leathers were clean and neat, hanging from a hook on the exterior of the wardrobe. Trin decided to be a little less rugged, and she put on the tight leggings and one of the dresses that Mirbella liked to make for her.

Her hair had twisted slightly when she slept, but a bit of brushing straightened everything out in a few minutes. She followed the custom of the dragons and kept her hair in multiple clasps without braiding it. Her white hair offset the gem tones that Mirbella chose. Anything pale just washed her out.

She pulled on her boots, shook out her skirts, and concealed three blades in the corset pockets designed for easy access via nearly invisible slits in the dress.

Trin left her room and went in search of her host.

Apraxa was wearing a headset and

pacing back and forth while speaking in a language that Trin could only recognize as vaguely Asian in origin.

Without missing a beat, Apraxa smiled at her, nodded, and moved to the kitchen to prepare a tray, all while chatting to the person on the other end of the signal.

Trin followed her to the dining room, and she settled down to eat the snack that Apraxa had prepared while her friend continued the negotiation for whatever it was she was speaking about.

The meat, cheese, and crackers told Trin that they were going out for a proper meal as soon as the call was over. A checking of her internal chronometer told her it was near six, so dinner was definitely in the cards.

She ate and drank her way through the tray and was nearly finished when Apraxa finished her call and removed the headset with a deep sigh.

"It doesn't matter that this is the twenty-first century, some men just do not like taking orders from women, so I had to get the supplier to put his mother on the phone. She agreed to my terms immediately but then spent the rest of the hour alternately insulting and then praising her son."

Trin smiled and offered Apraxa the last of the snacks. "She found out you were single."

"Something like that. They are fox shifters and notoriously difficult to deal with. The humans in their area and over here won't deal with them anymore, so I have to set the rules for outgoing transport and incoming goods."

"How did you get tapped for that?"

"I took Asian dialects in school. I muddle them up occasionally, but usually, when I am speaking to them, my brain keeps up."

Trin nodded.

Apraxa dropped into a seat next to her, and she smiled. "So, how long have you been a dragon?"

Trin blinked. "I beg your pardon?"

"Your demeanour, your new martial skills—not that your blade skills were lacking—and your fashion sense. Oh, and your hair. I have heard that the hair can change during the first transformation."

Trin debated admitting it, but something told her to just blurt it out. "Just about two months."

"You are human. You are marked as a human. There was no magic in you."

She wrinkled her nose. "Apparently, it was dormant. When another dragoness picked a fight, my dragon woke up. It was a really raucous baby shower."

Apraxa's eyes were wide. "You were *that* dragon? Wow. I read a short account of a new dragon appearing in the capital, but no one said who or how."

"It takes a dragon to wake a dragon. If I hadn't met that butt head, I would have remained a boring small businesswoman. My dragon has already picked her mate, and he is enthusiastic about the prospect. He's also really hot."

Apraxa laughed in surprise. "I never thought you would go for looks."

"He's more striking than handsome, is a librarian, and is on one of the con-

trol and recovery squads for the dragons. He is a good teacher. So is his
mom."

"You have a relationship with his
mom?"

Trin wrinkled her nose again. "Yes.
The details will have to remain vague,
but her son comes by his fighting skills
honestly."

"I need to learn more about this.
Dinner?"

"Sure. Name the place."

"Give me a minute, and we will go.
You are already dressed for it, but I look
like a bit of a slob." Her host disappeared around a corner.

Trin got up and paced a little, following a set of spiral stairs up and toward
the gusts of fresh sea air.

The view of the harbour was incredible. Ships that had a variety of propulsion techniques were making their way to the docks for unloading. This was where the east got all of their foreign goods. Everything travelled from this city, and it showed in the maze of roads, highways, and air travel that left the coast and headed inward and outward.

A pair of dragons was flying from the core to the interior with cargo in their claws. "Huh. I never thought of that."

"The dragons that fly cargo are the lowest caste. They are usually muddy greys and browns." Apraxa walked up to stand next to Trin, and she nodded toward an area where another set of dragons were loading off a high ridge. "They grab what their community has ordered and then drop off on the ridge to fly onward."

"Why not just take off?"

Apraxa gave her a slow smile. "Most don't have the strength. Do you?"

"No comment."

Her sea dragon is laughing quietly. Can you hear it? Trin's dragon whispered.

Trin cocked her head and listened with every part of her. She followed Apraxa down the steps and asked, "When did your dragon wake up?"

Apraxa paused at the bottom of the steps. "When my mother picked a fight at my twenty-first birthday. She grabbed me and hauled me into the ocean, and it was transform or die."

"Why did she try to kill you?"

Apraxa shrugged. "She really didn't. Her dragon could sense my dragon and wanted it out so that my mother's failure to find a mate could be offset by her being a mother to a strong female."

"It makes a difference?"

"Oh yeah. A daughter's strength adds to the mother's and raises her social position, at least in sea dragons." Apraxa shrugged.

Her elegant gown was slightly more formal than Trin's, but the shifting pattern of colour in it made it more eye-catching. "Come on, we have reservations, and our transport is waiting."

"So, you have been a dragon all this time?"

They were walking out of the house and through the warehouse before she answered. "Yes. It doesn't seem to be an issue."

"Your family knows?"

Apraxa shook her head. "Lords no. My brothers are happy sharks, and they think I am a beloved half-sister. They just think I am a little more cunning than they are. My step-mom knows. It was something I needed to tell her, and it confirmed what she had guessed. It isn't every shark that can raise a dragon with excellent business sense."

Trin laughed. "I am guessing not."

The long, sleek karros that was waiting for them was a deep grey.

"Are we going to a prom?"

Apraxa cackled. "The owner owes me a favour, and I want to get it off my ledger."

Trin nodded, and they slid into the vehicle in turn. A moment later and they were on their way to the elegant and exotic heart of the city. Every species was represented, including some of the most exotic fey and the very common beaver shifters. Dragons ruled it all, but they knew the value in those around them. It was what kept them in charge across the new world. Power could come and go, but the idea of respect was eternal.

Trin enjoyed her dinner with Apraxa as they didn't speak of their particular inner beings but rather enjoyed the high point in the restaurant reserved for the senator of the region.

Several men and women looked at them during dinner, but Trin was now used to being a bit of an attraction. She kept up her end of the conversation and laughed as loud as she liked. It wasn't every day that she went out for a casual chat with the head of the import and export guilds of Breaker City.

Tomorrow would be for trade, but

tonight, there were cocktails to be had.

Chapter Nine

Ystine was waiting in line with the other vehicles that were getting ready to leave the city.

"Are we returning to the capital?"

"Not quite yet. We are driving escort on a shipment of construction supplies," Trin murmured inside her helmet as the gate began to swing open.

"Why?"

Trin grinned. "Because the driver doesn't want to go. It is a scary place, and he is freaked out at having to stay there overnight."

"Where are we going?"

She glanced back at the truck behind her and nodded as she engaged Ystine's motor. "The Delarm Valley."

The velo didn't ask her anything, merely rolled forward with traffic. Ystine didn't care that they were going to the place where Trin's existence had started. Well, it seemed likely that it was where her parents had come together. She wanted to know if there was anyone else. Family was an elusive focus for her, but unknown family could be the most fantastic and amazing gathering of beings ever created. Or, they could be complete assholes. Trin looked forward to finding out.

Two breaks and ten hours of driving later, she pulled up to the gate for the Delarm Valley. There was one road.

Nothing else allowed entry to the town below.

The guard looked at her and tapped his head. She removed her helmet.

He turned white as a sheet and stepped back. "Why are you here?"

She blinked slowly. "I am driving escort for this shipment of materials from the city. The driver was nervous."

The guard blinked and ran a hand through his sandy hair. "Can I see a manifest?"

She reached into the pocket inside her leather coat. "Here you go."

He read through the list and swallowed nervously at awkward intervals. "Right. It looks like it is in order. Go down the road to the right. The Anders farm is on the right."

She quirked a smile. "Anders farm?"

"Yes. You look like the youngest daughter."

She nodded and looked to the driver, giving him a thumb's up. His expression was relieved, and his engine rumbled as he switched gears. Trin put her helmet on and nodded to the gate guard as he lifted the bar that had blocked progress.

She noted the bands in the road and saw the small units on either side. This road wasn't guarded by just a metal bar and a human. There was enough power accessible to toast her and Ystine into a smouldering pile, and it was right under her tires. She drove into the valley at a slow and sedate pace.

The valley was quite pretty, but her dragon was on alert. The place had the highest concentration of dragons outside the hub at the capital.

She followed the directions and drove slowly down the rough road to the farmhouse in the distance.

A small army was there to meet them when they arrived, and the men went to the rear of the truck while the women approached the driver and then Trin with lemonade.

She kept her head down but lifted her visor. "Thank you."

She took the straw between her lips and tasted the beverage made from fresh lemons and honey. "It's good."

The women chuckled. One said, "Thomas said you were a woman."

"He is correct."

One of the skirts at the edge of her field of view swayed slightly. "Will you stay the night?"

She glanced behind her. "Is the driver

getting the same invitation?"

The women murmured quietly, and the one who had spoken said, "No. Thomas said you looked like you were one of ours, so we wanted to find out."

"What is your name?"

"Meadra. Meadra Anders. I am the next bride."

Trin thought for a moment and then removed her helmet, turning to extend her hand toward the woman that looked like a slightly younger version of herself before the dragon bleached her.

"Trin Lem. Pleased to meet you."

The women standing behind Meadra paled, and one of them screamed. The men came running to find out what the problem was.

Meadra smiled and extended her hand. "Pleased to meet you, Trin."

There was a strange electricity when they made contact but nothing hostile. The smile was genuine.

An older man pulled Meadra away from the handshake. "Who are you, woman?"

She cocked her head. "My name is Trin Lem. I was born after my mother was torn to pieces by a dragon. Investigation leads me to believe that she once lived here."

The man stared and looked at her as if he was trying to tear her apart with his gaze.

Trin got off Ystine, and when she heard the closure of the truck, she gave the driver a nod. She was fine. He could go.

The truck rumbled along and turned around in the yard. Trin was still standing in a relaxed manner while the Anders family stared at her.

When the truck left, she cocked her head at the patriarch. "I am assuming that you are the elder Anders?"

The man blinked and scowled. "Who was your mother?"

"I am not quite sure, but the name LeeHee has been brought up. Do you know her?"

The entire family gasped and stepped back.

Meadra blinked and looked at the elder. "She's family, Father."

Her grandfather glared at her while he gritted out, "She is a mistake. She is not part of the pattern."

As she stared at him, his eyes flickered, and a muddy grey dragon gaze was looking at her. *This is just getting weirder.*

She didn't answer her dragon. It was hiding deep inside to conceal all traces of power.

"So, you have met dragons before."

Trin smiled slightly. "I live at the capital. The dragons there are distinctly in charge, but they also flick their eyes like that when they lose their tempers."

He blinked and leaned back. "You consort with dragons?"

"Yes. I have a shop, and they are frequent customers. Consorting is a little off though."

The men who looked to be in their forties and fifties were standing behind their father. Their wives slowly moved to be at their sides. Meadra was on her own.

Trin smiled brightly. "Are you my

grandfather?"

He frowned. "If you are LeeHee's daughter, you are my grandchild."

"How do we find out if that is true?"

"There is a seer in town. He can see the truth."

"Great. When can we see him? Oh, and what is your name?"

The elder crossed his arms over his chest. He might be pushing seventy, but he was in fairly fit shape. "You don't speak to me with respect."

"You don't speak to me with it either. I give what I get." She cocked her head. One of the men behind their father smiled slightly as if he had heard her phrase before.

He turned to the side. "Merrick, call Linder. Tell him that we have LeeHee's daughter here. He will trip over himself to get here."

Trin waited, and then, she looked at Meadra. "So, should I head into town to check records or something?"

The elder turned around. "You are staying here until I say otherwise. Your mother put generations of effort into jeopardy with her infatuation."

She sighed and loosened her coat, exposing the human marking at the base of her neck.

The family took a deep breath in shock, and Meadra walked up to touch the marking. "You are pure human?"

"Yeah. I was marked as a teen. It is just safer that I was considered an endangered species. The ports and cities are fine, but the dark alleys can be dangerous for someone like me."

Her grandfather looked at the mark

and hissed, "Human? That is impossible."

"Impossible or not, here I am."

Meadra looked from Trin to her elder, and she took Trin's hand. "Let's get you some more lemonade. We grow the lemons here."

Trin walked with her toward the house, but Meadra veered off and walked around the building and through a small gap in a hedge. Trin wanted to stop and stare, but she had to keep going. Her dream garden was arrayed before her in neat rows and permanent greenhouses.

"Wow. This is amazing."

"This is why people still deal with the valley. We have created a microclimate that grows fruits and vegetation from around the world for tisanes and herbal medicines." Meadra kept walking, and she led Trin to the second of the glass-paned greenhouses.

Inside, Meadra leaned toward her and whispered, "You have to leave."

Trin cocked her head. "I just got here."

"It isn't safe. If you are truly nothing but a human, you are as good as dead."

"Why?"

Meadra quickly looked back toward the home and whispered, "This valley exists to manufacture dragons. If you are a human, the plan has failed. They can't have you live if anyone learns of your situation."

"Wow. That is rather harsh." She asked a question that had been nagging at her. "Where is my grandmother?"

"She died birthing me. I wasn't even

supposed to exist, but LeeHee left, and they needed another girl for the program."

The door to the greenhouse opened, and one of the brothers was standing there. "Why did you run off with our guest?"

Trin smiled. "I showed an interest in the lemons. Meadra wanted to show me the greenhouses before the light faded."

The brother frowned. "That seems likely. Why would you have an interest in the greenhouses?"

"I have a partner in a business, and we sell coffee and tea. I always wondered why I had such a fascination with teas of all kinds, and now, I guess it was in the blood." She smiled.

"You have a tea store?"

She reached into one of the pockets of

her coat and handed him a card. "We have three coffee and three tea shops. We are working on expanding."

He looked at her in surprise. "You weren't lying."

"No. I don't lie. It wastes time."

He nodded. "I am your uncle, Rainer. My wife, Leda, was the one holding the pitcher."

"I am glad to meet you, Uncle Rainer."

He grinned. "It is definitely interesting to meet you. Your cousins will be at the morning meal so you can meet the herd then."

Meadra chuckled. "Each of your four uncles has three children. It makes for very loud breakfasts."

Rainer inclined his head. "The seer is on the way. He didn't hesitate when he learned who it was."

Meadra sighed. "Of course not. We will be right there."

Trin murmured the moment he was gone, "What is wrong with the seer?"

"He was your mother's fiancé, and now, he is mine. I am not just her sister, I am her clone. Someone had to keep the pattern going, so my mother was forced into a late pregnancy. She didn't make it."

With that echoing in her mind, Trin had to join her estranged family as they prepared to greet the seer. This was even more messed up than she had imagined.

They have surrounded you. The dragon growled.

I am aware of it.

Let me at them. I will tear them apart.

They are our family. We need to hear them out. Remaining calm while all the hair on her body was standing on end was difficult.

What will our mate think?

Well, I am due to make my calls in just over an hour. I will hint to him then.

That was all that she was allowed to say to herself. They had made it to the farmhouse, and she was ushered inside, and Meadra sat next to her on a loveseat.

One of the women brought in a tea service, but Trin was the only recipient of a cup. The rest of the family were seated with their spouses, and the elder frowned at her with flickers of softness in his expression.

She sat with the tea in her cup; the scent brought her the hints of a sedative and the brightest of summer apples. It was not a blend she favoured.

She broke the silence with, "Well, this explains my fascination for tea."

Her uncles jolted. Rainer looked at her with narrowed eyes. "Are you sure you didn't know about us before you arrived?"

Trin quirked her lips. "I knew the name Anders and my mother's name. That is it. I still don't know who *he* is." She gestured to the elder. "The tea is the best part of this visit so far."

Meadra chuckled.

A knock at the door stopped her aunt's laugh in mid-sound.

Trin's grandfather went to the door, and he spoke with the man who had just arrived.

Meadra was vibrating with so much tension that the loveseat was humming.

Trin gave her a quick glance, and the tension that her body was emitting was not on her face. Her face appeared placid.

The man that followed Trin's grandfather into the room was only younger than the elder Anders by a handful of years.

The seer was bent with rumpled clothing. He came toward Trin and grabbed for her hand, so she dumped the drugged tea on him.

He hissed and pulled his hand back. "Be careful!"

"Why? No one touches me without my consent." She rose to her feet.

He looked her in the eye, and then, he glanced at her grandfather. "Eamon, how am I supposed to read her if I can't touch her?"

Trin snapped her fingers in front of the seer's face. "You are supposed to ask. I swear. The Delarm Valley is the rudest place I have ever been."

She looked around at the shocked faces. "I need to make a call."

With long strides, she was out the door and down the porch steps in seconds. She checked her com and was unsurprised to see a lack of signal. That was fine. Ystine was able to generate what she needed; Trin just needed a moment away.

"Ystine, fire up. This place is crazy."

The velo was where she left her, and she swung onto the seat, and her companion helped her make her escape.

"I am guessing that your reunion was tense." The voice was amused as she followed the path through the farm and down to the township beyond.

"You could say that. They wanted a seer to check to make sure that I was LeeHee's daughter."

"So, now we are running?"

"Yes."

"You saw the barriers at the front gate?"

"Yup."

"So, what is the plan?"

Trin glanced skyward and saw the dragons above them. "I am working on it."

Chapter Ten

Three quick calls calmed Creata and Brenner. But Brommin was sent into a frenzy.

"Get out of there now, Trin. Shift and fly out if you have to."

"I think that my aunt needs my help."

"You have known her for five minutes." He was muttering.

"I know, but I get the feeling that having her with me is important. I don't want to leave without her."

She leaned as they swung around a fencepost and Ystine drove across a field.

The thudding of landing dragons ahead of her sent Ystine into a sharp spin.

"You have to get out of there. We have documents about a cult in that area."

"I can confirm that there are a lot of muddy dragons around here. There are four in front of me, so I have to change directions. I will call you in two hours if everything goes right."

"Wait, don't hang—"

She put her complete focus into driving Ystine through the gap in the dragons. Her uncles stepped back in reflex as the velo roared at them, and she passed through their blockade without trouble.

She was moving with a plan, and that plan got clearer as the signal went out and lesser dragons rose from the village. Nearly fifty dragons were tracking her movements as she looked around. She found what she was looking for and pulled her invisibility over herself while heading for a ridge in the middle of the field.

Ystine whispered in the helmet, "What is going on?"

"I am hiding us. I didn't know if I could hide you as well, and I am really glad I can. Now hush, I have to concentrate."

She drove them to the top of the ridge, and then, she waited.

The dragons formed a slow twister over her head, but she focused on the invisibility and remained still. Males. Every single flying dragon there was a man. Not one female was in search of her, and that was weird. Females were much better hunters. Farmers would know that.

Trin looked back toward the Anders' home, and it was alive with light. She made a quiet call and sighed when the answer was yes.

Trin set Ystine loose, and they flew off the ridge, invisibility gone, and Trin's focus was on getting Meadra. There was something in Meadra's eyes that made Trin want to protect her. Clone of her mother or not, Meadra was family.

The dragons were still swirling over the ridge and hadn't decided on what to do.

Trin focused on heading back to the farm. She pulled in front of the steps, and Meadra was standing there with her sisters-in-law. "Do you want to stay here?"

Meadra's eyes grew wide. "No."

"Get on."

Her aunt scrambled off the steps before her in-laws could catch her. When Trin felt arms around her waist, she sped away from the farm.

"Turn left!" Meadra shouted it.

Trin followed her order and the three that followed. A tiny, broken shed was leaning against a tree.

"Stop here. I will get my bags."

Trin blinked behind her visor and watched as Meadra sprinted to the shed. She was out in ten seconds with a backpack and a shoulder bag. It was ten seconds too long. The dragons were nearly on them.

Trin got off Ystine and fastened her

helmet to the paniers. "Hang on to your bags tight. This is going to be a little rough. I don't normally carry cargo or passengers."

Meadra stared. "What?"

Trin backed up a few steps, and she shifted. Her crystalline-clear body stretched and swelled until she was at her full size. She roared loud and long, scattering the dragons in every direction.

With careful motions, she picked up Meadra, and when she was secure, her right claw picked up Ystine. Her wings pulsed in the air, and she took off, knocking the few dragons who had returned to the area.

She held Meadra against her chest, and as soon as she had gained enough altitude, she went invisible. Her destination was firm in her mind. She was heading to Breaker City.

Trin got to the coastline and flew along the waterline. The journey that had taken the velo ten hours was accomplished by air in one.

She saw the signal from the air and flew toward the roof of Apraxa's home. In the first pass, she set Ystine down in the yard, and in the second pass, she set Meadra down carefully and then settled on the roof before shifting back to human.

Apraxa was staring. "You are a..."

"Crystal dragon. I know."

Apraxa shook her head, but Meadra muttered it from the floor of the rooftop. "Diamond dragon. You are what they have been trying for."

Trin moved to Meadra's side and

held her bluish fingers. The altitude that their travel required was not comfortable for most humans.

Apraxa was staring. "Did you say diamond dragon?"

Meadra nodded. "We were told about it. Eleven generations of dragons and humans with the most magic that could be found. One generation mates with humans and the next are born dragons. Girls are produced to mate with the dragons, and they carry the line within them. They wanted to create a male diamond dragon, but the odds were nearly impossible."

Apraxa lifted Meadra in her arms and carried her into the house.

"I will be right there. I have to put Ystine away." She shifted into her warrior form and walked to the edge of the roof, jumping off and gliding to land next to her velocipede.

With a grunt, she pulled her companion upright, and she patted the seat. "Well done, Ystine. You only screamed twice."

"I was not expecting to be flown across the continent," Ystine grumbled her disgust in her particular tone of voice.

Trin grinned and pushed her vehicle toward the warehouse. The wide door sensed her approach and slid open to allow her to place Ystine in her safe little energy shield. "I promise to wash you in the morning."

"Thank you. It was interesting to watch you tonight. I didn't know that I had cloaking properties."

Trin patted the seat and grabbed the

bags out of the paniers. "You don't. I do."

She slung her bag over her shoulder and headed toward the house in the back corner while the huge door clanged shut and locked.

It was time to get a nice, relaxing shower and take care of her aunt.

Wrapped in one of Apraxa's robes, Trin walked to the living room where Meadra was sitting with a strangely familiar mug between her hands.

Apraxa was sitting there quietly, and Meadra paused to wipe tears from her eyes.

"Meadra, is something wrong?" Trin walked up to her and sat beside her.

"I didn't actually think I would get free. I was getting married in two days when I turn twenty-four. I didn't want him touching me."

Apraxa cocked her head. "Him?"

Trin answered, "The seer. He was originally my mother's fiancé, but she got out as well."

"Oh. Ew." She wrinkled her nose.

Trin nodded. "Oh, did you get hold of Brommin?"

"Yes, he didn't want to take my call until I explained what you were doing. He should be here within the hour."

Trin nodded. "Excellent. I am not that good at this sort of thing. Hey, is that a sample mug?"

Apraxa laughed at the redirected topic. "Yes. He was so happy about how it turned out he wanted to get your final approval before the full run."

"Oh. Are there others?"

Apraxa got up and left the room.

Meadra clutched Trin's arm. "Can we trust her?"

"Apraxa? Yes. She is an old friend and trading partner. Half the city is terrified of her. No one is getting in here without her knowledge."

"But you trust her to know about the valley?"

Trin nodded. "I do. She has what she needs and is not currying favour with the dragons of the capital."

Meadra sighed and set her mug down before grabbing for her bags. "I have something here I think you will like. I found them when I was a child."

Trin didn't know what to expect, but the bound collection of books wasn't it. "Uh. Thank you."

"They are LeeHee's diaries. They

were hidden under a floorboard in my room." Meadra paused. "Which, I suppose, was her room."

Trin looked at the stack and slowly reached out to take them. "You kept them?"

"As soon as I could find a safe place for them, I moved them, but when I knew I had to leave, I made sure that they were set to come with me. The senator needs to know what is going on there."

Trin nodded and ran her fingers over the mismatched diaries and journals in her hands. "He does. I am not even sure what was happening there, but even at a glance, it wasn't good."

Meadra shuddered. "No, it was not."

Apraxa returned with a box in her arms. "Here you go, Trin. The family was very proud of the samples."

Trin blinked. "How did you know I would be back?"

"I guessed." Apraxa winked.

Trin scowled. "You are too clever for your own good."

"I know. Now, take a look at these designs. She really outdid herself."

Trin set the books down, patted Meadra on the shoulder, and then, she dove into the box, hands first.

The first thing she pulled out was another seasonal mug that depicted spring instead of the autumn that Meadra was holding.

The delicate, pale wisps of petals blew across the surface of the glossy ceramic. Trin turned the cup over and over, and there was no flaw or bubble in the cup or the glaze. "This is lovely."

"Their ceramics shop is a bit of a recent start, but I brought you there for a reason. Their talents and passions lie in the ceramics and not the import and blending of tea. You can help them reach the capital, and from there, the world."

Trin nodded, but she was cradling her new favourite teapot in her hands. It was smooth with a wide belly and graceful handle. The design was several gradations of blue and grey, working up to an ecru and blue sky with curls of snowflakes swirling through them. "This is amazing. It is exactly what I was looking for."

Apraxa chuckled. "Good. If you and Meadra are up for it, I would like to take you back to the market for some gift boxes that will fit the new line of ceramics and possibly gift tins for the tea."

Meadra perked up. "Shopping? In public?"

Apraxa nodded. "Shopping, in public. The more you are in public, the less chance you will end up missing. We need folk around here to recognize you, and that means that you need to be seen."

Trin looked away from her new treasure, and she smiled. "You can borrow some of my clothes. No one will recognize you."

Apraxa clapped her hands. "Ah! We can go shopping. That will be fun."

Meadra looked at both of them, and a tear ran down her cheek. She wiped it away, but they still lunged in and hugged her.

Trin said, "If you want to go back,

you can go back, but if you want to stay out here, you have options."

Meadra sniffed and nodded. "Yes. It has just been a wild day. Your flying was smooth, by the way."

Trin laughed. "I have had to do drills to figure out how the wings and tail work together. She does most of the work, but I have to figure out where we are going and how high."

Apraxa blinked. "That reminds me. How the hell can you be a diamond dragon? They are mythical, even for high-ranking dragons."

Meadra straightened and nodded. "That is the point of the program. The diamond dragon can—in theory—control other dragons. This is the philosopher's stone of dragons. They are said to be indestructible, enormous, and they have mastery of all around them."

Trin looked to Apraxa, and she grinned. "It isn't a flattering description, but I have been known to get my way on occasion."

Apraxa snorted and cackled, turning a golden blue before slumping onto the couch. When she sobered, she agreed. "Once or twice."

Trin was about to tuck Meadra into the room she had used previously when there was a familiar feeling in the air. She ran up to the roof and watched Brommin's dragon form come in for a landing.

He settled on the roof, and his sharp head turned toward her, sniffing her and sending her robe flapping around her legs. Trin leaned into him and stroked his hard beak, turning into an embrace of the man himself when he transformed.

"Thank the scales you are safe." He held her tight.

She leaned up and kissed him, holding his head as she greeted him properly. When she pulled back, she said, "What took you so long? Did you have to fight weather?"

"I had to fight my mother."

Trin leaned back further. "What?"

"She wanted to come in my stead. She thought I would be less obvious than she was."

Trin glanced over her shoulder where Apraxa and Meadra were staring at them. "Oh, yeah. You are barely visible at all."

Brommin gave her a slow look. "There is quite a bit of you on display, so thank you for that."

She looked down, blushed, and pulled her robe together. "It was your fault for the messy downdraft."

He kissed her quickly, and then, he murmured, "Would you care to introduce me to the ladies staring at us?"

"Right. First things first. We have to put out the beacons. Don't want any other dragons landing here and ruffling my robe."

Brommin chuckled, and they moved to the corners of the roof, putting out the marking lights. When the roof was dark, and the only illumination was the city, they headed back into Apraxa's hideaway and discussed the events and insane dragons of the day.

Chapter Eleven

eadra was staring at Brommin with fascination, and Trin let it go on for three minutes before she snapped her fingers between them. "Knock it off, Meadra, or my dragon will express her displeasure. He is hers."

Brommin sat on the couch next to Trin. "I don't mind being stared at."

Trin tapped him on the hand. "You are the first proper dragon that she has seen. I don't want her imprinting on you."

Meadra chuckled. "Not true. I saw you, and I have definitely memorized every part of you."

Trin grinned. "Right. Brommin, what do you know about diamond dragons?"

He picked up her hand and kissed the back of her wrist. "I know I am holding onto the only one I—or anyone else in the capital—have ever seen. The alchemist finished her tests. It was the reason I was frantic to keep you from being captured."

"Oh. That would explain it. So, what can you tell me about... well... me?" She turned her hand and cupped his cheek.

"The last recorded diamond was over two thousand five hundred years ago. She ruled a small kingdom on the African continent. When she chose to die, she shattered into pieces that seeded themselves in the ground with the curse of chaos lying with them."

Trin blinked. "Wow. I don't know if I like the exploding idea."

"We have traced mentions of diamond dragons around the world. Where you find diamonds, you find the resting place of one of the rarest dragons we have ever heard of."

She stroked his slightly stubbled cheek with her thumb and pulled her hand down to her lap. "Delightful."

"Some folks associate diamonds with love and eternity. I suppose that it is because, throughout history, the diamonds have only ever given up life when they have no mate."

Trin looked at him, and her dragon showed her a flash of their future together and her life after that with their children and their children. Life alone stretched on until it was time to let it go.

Brommin was holding her, and she focused on his features.

"Trin, what just happened?"

"I know why they would shatter." She let the slow tears of loneliness fall down her cheeks.

He pulled her onto his lap and simply held her while the other two looked on.

Feeling hundreds of years in a moment took a lot out of her. She leaned her head against Brommin's shoulder, and she sighed. "Apologies for that. Sometimes my dragon shows me things that I am not ready for."

Meadra stared. "It is a separate entity?"

Brommin answered. "Yes. The gemstone dragons have so much power that we require a secondary processing device. To control a shape so large would be impossible without more controlling power."

Apraxa grinned. "Try swimming. Your body is going in half a dozen directions at the same time."

Brommin looked surprised, and Trin realized she hadn't made the proper introductions.

"Master archivist and retrieval team leader, Brommin Lefarge, this is my friend, Apraxa Tiburon, and my—uh—aunt, Meadra Anders."

"Ladies, I would stand, but I am weighed down." Brommin inclined his head.

Apraxa coughed. "Lefarge? As in Senator Lefarge?"

Brommin inclined his head again. "Just so."

She looked to Trin. "Why didn't you say anything?"

"It didn't come up." She yawned. "Thanks for finding a shipment going to Delarm, by the way. I might have gotten in, but it would have looked a lot less spontaneous."

Meadra blinked. "You knew what you would find?"

She wrinkled her nose. "Not exactly. I have the updated autopsy file. I know how old she was and what physical condition she was in when she died. I also know that neither she, nor anyone else from the Delarm Valley, appears on a census. There is no record, and that means they are hiding something."

Meadra nodded, and then, she swayed.

Apraxa smacked herself in the forehead. "I am such a bad host. Come on, Meadra. I will put you in the room next to Trin."

Meadra nodded and followed Apraxa with soft *good nights* to Trin and Brommin.

Trin tried to move off her intended's lap, and he wrapped his arm around her.

"Tell me how many and what kind of dragons you saw today."

She wrinkled her nose and told him how many, what colours, and where they were located. "Oh, and the one road in is wired to electrocute something your dragon's size. There was no way I was getting across it with my velo."

"So, they don't want folk escaping."

"I am guessing that is the case. It is

why Meadra needed help."

Brommin nodded. "Is it weird that she is the precise image of your mother? Not close. It is exact."

"I know. She said she was a clone, but I thought you needed a high-tech facility for that."

His posture was suddenly rigid. "What do they grow in the valley? Trees, bushes? Are there a lot of hills?"

"No. It is very flat with only a small ridge of hills around the edge of the farmland."

"What grows on the ridges?"

She thought about it. "Close-cropped grass."

"Their facility is underground. I need to leave."

Trin sighed and got to her feet. "Fine. Just one thing before you go — mmf!"

His kiss was quick, fiery, and promised the future that she had just seen. He murmured, "The senate needs to know."

"I know. Go. I will stay in Breaker City until the ball. Visit if you can." She stroked his cheek and watched him sprint up the steps for a jumping takeoff from the roof.

She heard him leave and felt it as well. When Apraxa returned, she was rather surprised to find him gone.

"What the hell? Did you tell him you weren't going to put out?"

Trin was staring at the bookshelf. "No, he just saw that I haven't shaved my legs in a decade and ran for it."

"Funny. Where did he go?"

"He has to make a report to the senate and probably the more clandestine parts of the dragon council. They have to find out what is going on there."

"At the valley?"

"Yes."

Apraxa chuckled. "You don't really think that they are making a super dragon over there, do you?"

Trin stared at her and then pointed to herself.

"Oh. Right. Damn. I am so used to thinking of you as a tea and coffee merchant. Deadly dragon doesn't seem to fit."

"I know. I think that right until I see my hair in the mirror, and then, I remember, and she laughs at me."

Trin tightened the sash of her robe. "It has been an adjustment."

"I will put away the samples, and if you are happy with them, we can swing by the shop tomorrow."

"That sounds delightful. Thank you for everything." Trin gave her a hug and paused. "You don't think they can find us here? I flew with invisibility, didn't touch the seer, and never mentioned this city. Hopefully, they don't make their way here."

"They might split their forces and cover Breaker City and the capital. You are not going anywhere alone for the foreseeable future."

Trin pinched the bridge of her nose. "I had a feeling someone was going to say that."

Trin gave a few brushes and tugs to the clothing that Meadra was wearing and had to pronounce it a creepily good fit.

"You know, considering that this was tailored for me, it is an exceptionally good fit." Trin straightened and cocked her head. "The purple looks better on you than on me."

Meadra was touching the chaste but flashy expanse of her collarbone. "I have never worn anything like this. Is it new?"

"It was a few weeks ago."

Meadra touched it as if was made of gold. "I haven't ever had any clothing that hadn't seen five wearers before me. This fabric is so thick!"

Trin watched her aunt spin slowly and revelling in the simple joy of a dress with leggings and boots.

"You can spin later. Apraxa has found us another seamstress, so I can order a wardrobe for you."

Meadra stopped and looked at her with wide eyes. "I don't want you to spend all your money on me."

"You won't even make a dent. I have quite the nest egg." She wrinkled her nose. "So to speak."

"If you are sure... I wouldn't mind a few new corsets. This one fits like a dream. There are weird lumps in it, though."

Trin grinned and went up to her aunt, lining up the invisible slits in the dress with the corset and removing the blades. "Sorry about that. I load the corsets after they have been cleaned."

"You carry knives?"

Apraxa spoke from the doorway. "She does. Knows how to use them, too."

Meadra cleared her throat. "Can I

keep one?"

Trin blinked and nodded. "Sure. Hold still. It is harder to get them in when you are dressed. I don't want to stick you."

Meadra nodded, and Trin slid the easiest-to-access knife in place. Lower center front, next to the busk. The steel in it helped hold the knife motionless.

The next five minutes were spent showing Meadra how to withdraw the knife. They were a few minutes late heading out for brunch, but the diner had their table ready and waiting.

Apraxa's brothers fawned over them and got Meadra anything she wanted. Trin was surprised by the effect she was having, but her dragon was accepting this as normal. It was only proper that someone with the genetics of Trin's mother should be exhibiting the attraction characteristics of a dragoness reaching her first season.

Trin didn't bother arguing that her mother hadn't been a dragon, so it was doubtful that her aunt was. Explaining their relationship was difficult, so they had decided on introducing her as a cousin.

Apraxa sipped her tea and smiled. "It seems your *cousin* is very popular with my brothers. Does she know what a shark is?"

Trin shook her head. "I am fairly sure that she doesn't. Damn. I should have thought of this."

"What?"

Trin leaned forward and whispered, "I read my mom's journal. Her fling wasn't an accident or a whim of true love, she wanted out, and she thought that Lord Millet could take her away. She didn't particularly want him, but she was willing to use sex to ensnare him."

Apraxa whistled. "Wow. That is a tale as old as time."

"When she confronted her father and mother, they ordered her to marry the seer anyway. They would simply dispose of the baby. They watched her day and night for the next seven months."

Apraxa leaned forward and propped her chin on her hands. "Then what?"

Trin blinked and swallowed. "She didn't run for herself, she didn't run for Lord Millet, she ran for me. Every time I kicked, she knew I was bound to do things that she had never dreamed of."

"How did she get out?"

Trin shrugged. "I don't know. I only have the journal entry from the day before she ran. She went through a few plans, but I don't know which one she actually carried out."

"Of course. Did you meet your grandmother?"

The swish of skirts pulled up next to their table as Meadra rejoined them. "No. Her grandmother died having a baby at sixty-two years old."

Apraxa blinked. "Why did she do that?"

Meadra arranged her skirts as she sat. "Because LeeHee was their obligation child. They had to have a daughter, so when she left, they had to have another. Maintaining the pattern was imperative. They would lose their standing in the community and in the project."

Trin cocked her head. "Ah. That. I am pretty sure that that is going to require a chat with someone with high security clearance."

"Right. I am just so excited to be able to speak in a regular conversation, I got carried away."

Trin patted her hand. "Finish your breakfast and remember the fascinating methods of making coffee, and we will be out in the market where you can chat with anyone you want."

Apraxa smirked. "I am going to be using your appeal to try and strike some bargains. Feel free to flirt at will."

Meadra blinked, and then, she smiled slyly. "I will do what I can."

Chapter Twelve

It was the first time Trin had ever had to hire a courier to take their packages back to Apraxa's.

Four hours of shopping later, Trin was definitely up for a cocktail and a nice lunch by the inland lake.

Apraxa's karros had been taken out of the warehouse for the journey into the depths of Breaker City, and it was only when Trin saw something that she recognized on a billboard that she flinched.

"Maybe we should just order in at your place."

Apraxa grinned and turned toward a display of banners and billboards that made Trin's cheeks heat. "But why? You look great in those ads."

"They weren't ads when I posed for them; they were just art photos with landscapes."

Meadra stared and said, "Trin, that is you! Your hair is so much darker."

Trin tried not to look at the images of her posing in fashion from history, from ancient Sumeria to modern day. The images had been sold and were now being used to advertise the Breaker City museum.

Apraxa laughed. "It is fine. It got you the money for the start-up, didn't it? You and Brenner were able to open your first shops with it."

"I know. I am just very happy that it

is confined to Breaker City."

"Yeah, you might want to check your royalty account. I am pretty sure that this campaign caught on."

Trin groaned.

Apraxa pulled into the lot next to the museum and turned off the vehicle. "We are here. Come on, we have reservations in the teahouse within the arboretum."

Trin got out and looked at her friend over the roof. "How do you get all of these reservations?"

Apraxa winked and didn't answer.

Meadra was excited by everything she saw. A whole new world had literally opened up for her. Trin focused and used patience, giving Meadra the information she needed to understand the world she was presented with.

The nine vendors and dressmakers they had seen that morning and dubbed Meadra to be her sister, and Trin was fine with that. Family was hard to figure out.

Meadra walked with her and whispered, "Why did you buy so much baby stuff today? Are you pregnant?"

Trin snorted. "No. That would get me shunned. I am just picking out things for my goddaughter. Since this city is a trading hub, it is easy to send things to the capital from here."

"Do you think that my father will trace me here?"

Trin linked arms with her and murmured, "He is using a seer, so we are going to have to use other methods to hide you."

Apraxa chuckled. "That is why we

are here. We are here to have your cards read and your aura disguised."

Meadra squeaked. "You can do that?"

"Me? Oh hell no. I know people, and those people know people. It has taken a while to gather everybody that I need to move through life calmly, but I am there now." Apraxa smiled slightly.

They walked along the crushed-shell path behind the museum, and when they rounded the corner, the two-acre greenhouse that was the arboretum reclined on the landscape with elegant tiers of glass reaching to fifty feet in height.

Trin was impressed. She had never been to the arboretum while she had lived in Breaker City. It had been far too expensive for her student wallet.

They walked up to the doors, and the attendants pulled the glass panels open to allow them inside. "Welcome to the arboretum."

Meadra smiled and chirped, "Thank you!"

Trin nodded to the men, and their group entered the warm and humid expanse.

A woman in an elegant day gown met them. "Reservations?"

Trin kept her witty banter to herself.

Apraxa smiled. "We are here for the curator's table."

The woman looked skeptical. "Name?"

"Apraxa."

The greeter blinked and bowed low. "Welcome to the arboretum. Please, come with me." She straightened and gestured in the direction she was going to take them.

They followed the woman through the lush, growing space. They walked toward a mural on the wall where a hidden wall panel opened, and the woman gave them instructions. "Simply press the only button in the elevator, and it will take you to the curator's table."

They nodded, and she returned to her station. They stepped into the small room lined with the same glass as the giant greenhouse around them.

Trin and Apraxa made sure that Meadra was comfortable, and then, Apraxa pressed the button that started the motion of their little room.

The lift moved on a diagonal, coasting up the wall and letting them have a delightfully thorough view of all of the levels.

Meadra was holding onto Trin's hand tightly, but her eyes were shining with delight. "When we are done with lunch, can we explore the gardens?"

Trin smiled at Apraxa's frown. "She's a gardener."

"Ah. Certainly. Yes, we can look through the gardens." Apraxa smiled, but there was a tension in her face.

The lift continued to rise on the diagonal, and when they arrived at the highest level, the chamber stopped moving, locked in place, and the door opened.

Trin led the way out and sighed inwardly when Meadra released her from the tight grip of her hand.

Apraxa smiled. "This way."

The level they were on was suspended above the main arboretum. The floor was as transparent as the walls around them, but a path had been created to make the walkway opaque.

Apraxa led them down the path, and soon, a platform rose up, and it contained a wide circular table and four chairs.

"Ladies, have a seat." Apraxa took a chair and settled.

Meadra sat across from her, and it left Trin sitting between them.

The moment they were all settled, a light chime went off, and a server appeared with a tea service. Apraxa's slight smiled let Trin know that this wasn't just a server.

As the woman set the tray down and she poured the tea, Apraxa smiled. "Thank you for seeing us, Curator."

"You are welcome, sea born." The woman smiled slightly. "It is an odd day when so many dragons collect in my private dining space."

"One of them is in immediate danger, so we are coming to you to hide her."

"Very well, first, drink your tea and pass me your cups. I need to check to see what the winds of time have planned for you." The curator sat back and lifted her own cup.

Trin and the others all picked up their cups and slowly sipped. The leaves pressed against her lips for a moment, but she was practiced at this and simply sipped the green tea until the cup was empty.

The curator beckoned, and Trin handed the cup over. With an expert swirl, the woman tipped the cup upside down on the saucer.

Trin waited, and when the curator lifted the cup, she sent a surprised look at Trin. "You have taken on the mantle?"

"It wasn't like I had a choice. I will be what I am and inhabit every part of it."

Meadra blinked. "Wow."

Trin winked.

The curator nodded. "You do seem surprisingly stable, considering what I see here. Well, if we have to have a new ruler that can override any dragon-run government around the world, I am confident that you won't go mad. Hold tight to those close to you."

"That makes one of us."

Apraxa slid her cup over to the curator.

The curator gave her a sly smile. "A

tempest is heading your way. You cannot avoid it. Decisions must be made, and you have to either embrace your future or dodge it as you have been doing."

"I have not been dodging it, I have merely been going over my options. Life in Breaker City is exhausting."

"Perhaps you should visit the sea more often. I am sure that you would be well received."

Meadra finished her tea and handed the cup over. The curator winked at her and took the cup. She swirled, flipped, and lifted the cup again, looking from the cup to Meadra to Trin and back again.

"Well, you are in danger from your past and your present. You need to stay close to your daughter and niece. She will introduce you to your destiny."

The curator paused. "You know that you are not human and not dragon, correct?"

Meadra nodded. "I suspected. They were taking far too many blood and tissue samples."

The curator nodded. "It makes a certain amount of sense. You can't stop female dragons from manifesting for generations and not have the magic that lets us shift implode."

Trin focused on what the curator said. She had said *us*. There was another dragon in their midst.

Meadra asked the question that Trin was waiting for. "What am I?"

"Human mythology hasn't been too focused, and our records are incomplete, but you are the beginning of a new species. There are magical or psychic humans in your bloodline?"

Meadra nodded. "Every other generation."

The curator exhaled and leaned back, placing her hands on the table. The glass under her hands took on the appearance of water, and ripples ran along the surface while the teacups remained in place.

Faces floated up from the table and hovered in the air in front of them all. The curator reached up and flicked aside the masculine faces, enlarging the female ones. She hissed slightly and tapped her lips with one finger while bringing the faces to the fore one by one.

"You are a copy of Trin's mother, yes?"

"Yes."

"You are also a copy of your grandmother, and great, great grandmother. They have been remaking you for the last two hundred forty years."

Meadra blinked. "Me?"

"Yes, you. Something in the early tests notified them that you were extraordinary. Now, we just need to find out how they did it."

She beckoned to the first image that looked a lot like Trin.

"Why does she look so much like me?"

"Her genetics were reinforced. Mendellian inheritance. Huh. They must have started it immediately."

Apraxa frowned. "That was only published in eighteen sixty-six."

The curator smiled. "That was the publishing date. It is a far older premise.

Unlike humans, shifters have known about the origins and mechanics of reproduction for nearly a thousand years. I really wish I could get a hold of the documentation of this project."

Meadra scowled. "I am not a project."

"Yes, you are. Trin is a mutation of the project. She was the result when someone added the wrong ingredient." The curator took the eldest image and did something with her fingers. Another bolt of female images cascaded upward.

Trin sat and watched the curator flick through the images of their ancestors. Meadra touched her hand and held it. They watched the history in their genes on display and the women who all had a striking similarity.

The sound of metal feet on the floor got Trin's attention. A mechanical automaton was approaching with a laden tray. Trin had never seen one that was the same size as a human before.

The metal butler set plates in front of each of them while the curator continued her study.

Trin and Meadra each took up a sandwich with their free hand and started eating.

Apraxa looked at them, grinned, and started her own lunch.

The curator continued her research until she reached an image that made her nod and smile. "Got it." She dismissed the images and flexed her fingers before taking a bite of her own before sighing happily. "That took a while. I apologize. Your line is ancient beyond what I could have guessed."

Apraxa paused as the automaton returned with tea. "Is their line that old?"

"It goes back to the last provable diamond dragon."

Trin held Meadra's hand. "What?"

"Dragons have siblings, and you are of a branch of the last diamond dragon's family. Descended from her aunt and raised in a tiny community, which is where the inbreeding started."

Trin recoiled. "What?"

The curator waved her hand. "It was very common in ancient times before anyone realized what the effect might be on the genes. Usually, enough new genes could be gained via travellers. That is where the breeding plan was first created, or that is my guess. Without documentation, I can't tell."

Trin blinked. "Well, that is something. Why are they focusing on the female line?"

The curator grimaced. "Without the ability to shift, the women are easy to control, so they simply stop the women from shifting until they link them to a mate who stops their instincts from rising."

When the automaton returned, Trin took a second cup of tea, but this one did not contain swirling leaves.

The curator smiled at the metal man. "Headly, could you get me the protection charm on my desk?"

The construction bowed and walked off.

The curator looked at them, and she rocked her head from side to side. "That was a little more activity than I had imagined. Do not get me wrong, I have enjoyed it, but I was surprised."

Meadra frowned. "So, what am I in danger from?"

"Your past. Your past is chasing you, and it wants you back. Your niece-daughter is your ticket to safety. Stay close to her."

Apraxa asked her own question. "Do you have a timeline on the tempest?"

"No, but it will be coming for you. I know you are ready for it, but things will go more easily if you can go to it."

Apraxa looked at Trin.

Trin smiled. "Do what you have to, we are fine. I can find a home for us until we need to head to the capital."

"You can stay at my house. I order you to stay at my place until you need to go back."

Meadra cleared her throat. "Will we be safe here? I mean, Trin flew in and

Brommin. What about my family just landing on the roof?"

Apraxa shook her head. "If I don't turn on the beacons, even Trin couldn't find it. She had to call ahead to get me to activate them. Over the years, I have paid for every type of protection for that space that I could. It is secure. You can rest there and look up what you need to. I have a pretty good library."

Trin nodded. "She does. Now, Apraxa, what is the tempest?"

Apraxa sighed and wrinkled her nose. "He's another dragon. Technically my fiancé by arranged marriage. My mother's family linked me to him when I was a child. He doesn't want a human, so I have been able to avoid him by not going to my grandfather's home for visits. Since my human form can't swim that well, I can't really get to the deep ocean without shifting."

Trin sighed. "Well, I promise not to wreck your house if you want to go and settle things with the tempest. Why is he called that?"

Apraxa shrugged. "He's a storm dragon."

"What are you?"

Her friend grinned. "I am a hurricane."

"That is absolutely appropriate."

The curator stood. "You two talk this out. Meadra, would you care for a tour of my gardens?"

Meadra was on her feet in an instant. "Yes, please. How long have you worked here?"

"I have been here since the gardens began."

Meadra looked around. "Some of these plants are two hundred years old."

"Are they? What a keen sense of flora you have. Come along."

The curator offered her arm, and Meadra linked her arm through that of the strange psychic. The automaton appeared again and handed the curator a small object that she passed to Meadra.

Trin turned back to her friend. "Do you know what the curator is?"

"She is old, she has been here since the city was founded, and she likes plants."

"She said she was a dragon."

Apraxa nodded. "I caught that, too. It makes sense."

"Does it? Very little about this makes sense, aside from me being sure that I will be there when they let me claim Brommin."

Apraxa cocked her head. "How did you know he was the one for you?"

"My dragon told me, in rather graphic detail. I also saw our entire lives together when I last saw him. It was heady and hard to watch, but I will enjoy our family."

"Did you see yourself in charge?"

Trin laughed. "You have known me for half a decade. I am always in charge."

Apraxa giggled, and she nodded. "There is that. Now, I don't want you two to have any parties, and no boys. Other than that, go nuts. I should be back home in a week."

"Do you need me to do anything for your business?"

"No, I will have my Tesla, and I get reception at my grandfather's home."

Trin reached out and squeezed her hand. "Good luck."

"You are going to need it more than me. You have to keep track of your mother who is going into heat and flirting with every man she sees. Enjoy."

Trin groaned and looked through the glass panels, seeing her excited aunt-mother flitting through the greenhouse with the curator. "I think we are going to be regular visitors here. I will buy a membership."

* * * *

The curator felt the gaze of the diamond dragon on her back. She smiled. There was going to be a riot of activity surrounded her in the next few months, but if she kept her resolve and remembered those around her, things would right themselves. Diamonds were known for their calm discretion, so it was likely that things would be all right.

The manufactured fey next to her was another matter. Those who had created her would not stop coming until she was either with them or beyond their grasp. If Meadra let Trin take care of her, things would work out for her, though her possibilities for a mate were so bizarre it didn't bear thinking of.

The curator was happy to stay with her plants. They understood her, and she protected them. It was so much easier than dealing with the regular population. People were draining, and seeing their timelines was exhausting.

Author's Note

Huh. The second instalment of whatever this series is is over. The next story *Dragon Engaged,* will not be released until 2019, and with the last chapter, I am not even sure which dragon it is.

Thanks for reading,

Viola Grace

About the Author

Viola Grace (aka Zenina Masters) is a Canadian sci-fi/paranormal romance writer with ambitions to keep writing for the rest of her life. She specializes in short stories because the thrill of discovery, of all those firsts, is what keeps her writing.

An artist who enjoys a story that catches you up, whirls you around and sets you down with a smile on your face is all she endeavours to be. She prefers to leave the drama to those who are better suited to it, she always goes for the cheap laugh.

www.ingramcontent.com/pod-product-compliance
Lightning Source LLC
Chambersburg PA
CBHW061300210726
48293CB00003B/1044